THE MASTER OF DEMISE

A DARK AND RIVETING PSYCHOLOGICAL THRILLER

NADIJA MUJAGIC

There are so many ways of being despicable it quite makes one's head spin. But the way to be really despicable is to be contemptuous of other people's pain.

JAMES BALDWIN

THE MASTER OF DEMISE

NADIJA MUJAGIC

CHAPTER 1

NOTHING GIVES *me a natural high like burning stuff, but killing comes close. This one was quick and painless.*

I come home, go to the bathroom and throw the gloves in the tub. Cheap, thin ones that people use when they clean their home. I light them on fire and watch them burn until they're ashes. I don't want to wake my wife, so I open the bathroom window and blow the fire smoke out of the room. She is not a light sleeper, but sometimes strange and unexpected smells or sounds can wake people up.

I clean the tub to remove all the ashes and the fire soot. I take all my clothes, including my mask, and put them in the hamper. No visible traces of murder remain on them, but I do it anyway for extra precaution. As I hit the sack, I'm thankful to find my wife on her back snoring away, with her mouth hanging open. I flip her to her side to stop the snoring and turn around to fall asleep.

But the adrenaline keeps me wired. My senses are still

heightened beyond what I'm comfortable with. I'm scared I won't be able to fall asleep, but then my eyes finally close.

When I wake up, I get ready for work, restless and tired. As soon as I show up, I'm given the news I was hoping for.

He is dead.

Everyone on the campus is talking about it: the students, the staff, the faculty. They all look distressed, unable to comprehend the sudden loss of a young, healthy man most people seemed to love.

People are whispering the news from every corner, shock shining from their eyes. I smile inside. I wish I could offer them comfort by saying that he swiftly arrived at his painless, predetermined end.

I'm doing everyone a favor. An immense relief washes over me as I think about how much better the world will fare with one fewer bully. He was the right target.

Now, I just wait and watch my actual victim's life fragment into pieces.

WEDNESDAY

CHAPTER 2

BRADFORD ROBERTSON WAS the second student to die this year.

This morning, around seven, his roommate found him at his desk in his dorm room, his head resting on the desktop next to a textbook. He was an excellent student, with a GPA average of 3.94 on the 4.0-point scale. His remarkable physical condition gave him the edge to be one of the best basketball players for the university team. When he strolled around the campus, you couldn't help but notice him. He exuded authority and a certain aura that made people surround him.

It didn't take long before the news of his death has spread throughout the small campus. Everyone now knows Bradford is gone. But the reason remains a mystery. Shock thrashes through the campus like waves in a storm.

His death was unexpected.

I'm checking emails in my office when William Harris

walks in. I've known William since our Harvard days, where we both served our postdoctoral appointments, but we haven't worked closely since he became the chair for humanities department a few years ago. He's been different ever since our initial meeting. There's something about being a department chair that brings on razor-sharp diplomacy and butt-licking—I guess I never suspected he'd be good at it, but he is.

His knuckles make the slightest of contact with my door before he comes in, his face a mask of anxiety. He hesitates at first, then greets me in a sour voice. "Hi, Mitch."

"Yes, William?" I say.

"Mitch." He sounds nervous. "The police are here and making rounds of interviews regarding Bradford's death. Just a routine procedure, they say. They will stop by your office this morning to talk to you."

"They will?" I look at him beyond the upper rim of my glasses. "I have nothing to do with this student's death. Why would they talk to me?"

He shakes his head and furrows his brows. "They found some evidence that he was stressed about his grades. Bradford has been almost a straight-A student until he took your psychosis class this semester. He has a C and a D. That's quite a surprise for a student of his caliber. They're just trying to understand if the grades might have led him to take his own life."

I stand up from my chair and walk toward William.

Like a vulture, I'm looping around the chair in the center of my office and studying the floor as I ponder. William is close to the door, observing my slow movements.

"Indeed. How would I not know?" My voice is on an even keel. The whole incident seems suspicious, but I'm not shaken by his announcement. I am calm. "There's no way he took his own life because of a C or a D. That would be absurd!" I stop and give William a stern gaze. His tall figure is standing near the door and swaying back and forth. He's staring at me and shrugging his shoulders. It's not common for William to be without words, but this time, it's undeniable.

"I don't appreciate you insinuating I'm the reason Bradford took his life." I tell him. "As for the grades, as far as I recall, his major was math. Sometimes hard science students don't have the aptitude for humanities, and vice versa. But the semester is still in full swing, and his grades are not final. He could still end up with a B plus if he worked hard."

If he were still alive, that is.

"They have found his diary this morning, and he has written some disturbing things in there." William says.

"A diary?" I pitch my voice high. "A man of his age writes a diary?" I scoff.

"Why is that so strange, Mitch? You, of all people, shouldn't be judging the young man and stereotyping."

I wave my hand and walk away, putting my back to him.

"Listen, Mitch. This is a second death on the campus within a year. It's troubling."

I hear panic in William's voice. He works tirelessly in his role as chair to maintain the university's standing and reputation. The passing of Bradford makes him anxious; the last student suicide caused a lot of trouble for the university.

Almost a year ago, a literature major student named Lauren Bisbee took her own life. She couldn't concentrate on studying after her boyfriend dumped her. It's unfortunate how these younglings get attached to men so easily. She'd failed class after class, and received poor grade after poor grade, causing her GPA to fall below 2.0. As a result, the university authorities asked her to pull out of the program. Two days after she received the letter, she hung herself in the dorm room. It wasn't until her friend asked where she'd been all day that they found her. Her friend walked into the room and screamed at the sight of Lauren hanging from the ceiling, lifeless.

Lauren's parents sued the university for negligence. They were an older couple, and Lauren was an only child. She was the heart of their lives and, while away at the university, they would call Lauren daily to check in on her and see if there was anything they could give her to bring her joy—maybe some money, or her favorite home-made jam, or sweaters her dad had knitted just for her. The love of her parents was not enough to bring her life back on track. The whole incident was truly unfortunate.

The court mandated the university to make free psychotherapy sessions and a suicide hotline available to students. The punitive damages have taken a toll on our university's small endowment.

I was among those in charge of devising the plan. The court also wanted us to run frequent, official tests to gauge students' state of mind: are they depressed? Anxious? Do they have a reason to get up in the morning? And things like that.

The Bradford's case seems different. I didn't detect any depression or distress from him, which differs from Lauren. This whole thing seems rather suspicious, but I don't argue.

I turn around and face William again. He crosses his arms, and I see sweat forming on his forehead. We're in the midst of autumn, and it's not overly warm in my office.

"These deaths are completely unrelated. But I acknowledge your concern." I walk around my desk and sit down in the chair.

William sits opposite me, even though I haven't invited him to stay. "I am concerned that the news will travel far, and our reputation is going to be ruined."

I nod at his statement.

Vermont University is known for its small size and the professor student ratio. Young people choose to come here because it feels intimate and friendly. The total enrollment for undergraduates is only a thousand, and half of them, if not less, are graduates.

"Indeed. But if the standards are raised, and no one expects to get nothing but As, maybe students will stop taking their own lives."

His face turns angry. "It's not as simple as that, Mitch. We educate our students, and I take pride in that. They work hard and they get what they deserve."

I'd rather not engage in a lengthy dispute with William. He has been good to me. He never said it directly, but I believe he was the one who pushed for my tenure two years ago. I am established in academia, which means I don't have to worry, thanks to him.

I say nothing. We sit in an awkward silence. William slams his palms against the armrests and stands up. "Anyway, I should get going." He looks at his watch, then at me. "The cops should stop by any minute now."

He turns around and rushes through the door. The loud slam startles me. I curse under my breath.

CHAPTER 3

I STAND by the window overlooking the small campus. The architecture of the buildings at the university never fails to amaze me. I often swivel in my chair to turn to the campus and enjoy the view. The library with the impressive Greek revival columns particularly inspires me.

Snow flurries in the air catch my eyes immediately. Winter comes early in Vermont. It's only mid-October. When it gets cold, the campus becomes ghostly, with just a few students rushing through the campus, from point A to point B. Since the news about Bradford broke, an invisible layer of sorrow has settled on the structures.

I make a step closer to the window and see the ambulance car parked outside in front of the building. I crane my neck, curious to see what's unfolding below. The wind is picking up and eating the flurries flying in the air. Two men wheel a stretcher out of the building. On top of it lies a covered mass—what I assume is Bradford's deceased body. The men carefully maneuver the stretcher—a task they have done many times—one of them opening the ambulance door in the back and jumping in. The other one is right behind, holding the stretcher on the other end and pushing it towards the car. Seriousness leads to wrinkles in his forehead. Seconds later, the ambulance car beeps as it moves in reverse. Then it drives away in silence.

Just as I sit down at my computer, someone knocks on my door. I keep it closed at all times, because foot traffic in the hallway can be intense. When I'm busy, I can't be distracted by people.

"Come in," I say.

The door opens, and two cops come in. William is behind them, looking like a child who's about to be reprimanded in a principal's office. He looks calm, but I know he is a nervous wreck.

"Here's Mitch," he says in a low voice.

The two cops enter with firm resolve and don't say a word. One is older, maybe in his fifties, and I remember him from the Lauren Bisbee case. He still looks the same, but with more gray hairs and sagging eyes. The other cop is maybe half his age and appears to be his protégé. They both look soft, not a mean bone in their body, but their faces are stern and serious.

I point at the two chairs across from me and I invite them to sit down. One does, and the other shakes his head and stands near my desk. Out of an old habit, I pull a comb from my inside pocket and run it over my hair once. They are both watching me while William is standing near the door, awkwardly.

"Do you need anything from me?" William asks.

The older cop turns to him. "No. We're good here. Thank you."

And then it's just three.

"How can I help you, gentleman?"

The older one, standing up, says. "This is Officer Moy, and I'm Officer Banks. How are you doing today, Professor Wegner?"

"Fine. I'm fine." I say.

Officer Banks is holding a notebook and resting his other hand on his waist, two inches from the pistol hanging on his belt. "How can I help you?" I ask again.

"We have a few questions about the student who was found dead this morning. Can you tell us a little something about him? Has he been your student for a long time?"

I lean deeper into the chair, cross my leg and put the fingertips together while pursing my lips and thinking. Thinking about Bradford. He had so much potential.

"Well. I've seen him around the campus before he took my class this semester. But until he enrolled in my class, no, I never interacted with the man." I prefer to be short and sweet.

"What kind of student was he, would you say?"

I uncross my leg and lean forward at my desk. "He

struck me as an ambitious and intelligent young man. Quiet. I don't think I heard him once speak during class."

"How big is your class?"

"The last enrollment number says forty-four."

"Forty-four. Do you expect your students to talk in a class that big?"

"It's not mandatory, but certainly encouraged. How are they supposed to learn if they don't ask questions and brainstorm ideas?"

"I don't know. You tell us."

I want to tell them my question was rhetorical, but I wonder if they know what that means.

"I've carried out research over and over to prove that speaking ideas, as opposed to only reading them, improves understanding of the subject at hand. I couldn't tell if Bradford had no interest in psychology or had no affinity for it. It is indeed difficult to make an assessment when the student remains mute in the classroom." I hope this will drive home with them. But they don't respond or say anything to my explanation.

"Tell us about your grading system, Professor Wegner? Would you say you are a stricter or more lenient grader?"

"I ... how is this question relevant?" I'm annoyed, and they can tell.

Officer Banks waves the notebook at me. "We found Bradford's diary in his dorm room. The day you gave him a D, he wrote an entry, and he has some interesting things to say about you."

He flips the pages and stops when he finds the entry he wants to share with me. He extends his arm with the diary in his hand and asks me to read.

Somewhat hesitantly, I take the diary and dart my eyes around the page.

I got my midterm back today. I got a D. A fucking D. What am I gonna say to my parents about this? I'm ashamed. This will totally ruin my GPA. I really hate this class. The only reason I'm taking it is because I need to take credits in humanities. If I knew this professor was going to be a dick, I'd have considered taking something else. Like Shakespeare. Or fiction writing. Anything to avoid this narcissistic egomaniac.

My eyes widen at the last sentence. I take a pause and reread it again. Narcissistic egomaniac. I've been called names before, but never this. Is that what students think of me? Now I wonder. I am not shaken or anything. I can't believe he never held me in high esteem.

I continue reading.

But it's too late now. If I withdrew from class now, it'd be late to take something else, and I don't want to take five classes next semester. I want to end this semester with sixteen credits completed. God, I wish someone had warned me about this asshole. How am I going to explain all this to my parents? My dad gets angry when I get anything below B+. If our professor wasn't such a stickler, things would be okay. He's my biggest nightmare. He doesn't belong in a classroom. MITCH BELONGS IN A DITCH.

I finish reading and hand back the diary to the officer. So, Bradford wanted me dead. They stare at me to see my reaction, but I have none. I wait for one of them to say something.

"Does any of this resonate with you?"

I smile. "No, not really."

Officer Banks tilts his head and narrows his eyes at me. "You're not bothered by what you just read, Professor Wegner?"

"Listen, everyone is entitled to their opinion. No one's view is absolute truth." I'm afraid I'm getting too philosophical, but I mean it. I don't care for Bradford's opinion.

"Professor Wegner, where were you last night?"

"Last night?"

They're taking Bradford's death from a different angle. Maybe his death wasn't accidental as they initially thought. Maybe it wasn't suicide because of poor grades. They're seeking an alibi from me, as if I'm the prime suspect.

But I have nothing to do with his death.

"I was home with my wife." I say. "We watched a movie and went to bed early."

Officer Banks looks at me and nods. Awkward silence ensues in the room. Officer Moy stands up and approaches my desk to stand next to Officer Banks.

"Would you say Bradford had any enemies at the school?" Officer Moy speaks up.

I make a face and consider the question. "I'm not privy to Bradford's social life, sir. That's something you can ask the students."

They nod at each other. "Before we take off, is there anything else you want to share with us? Anything else you want us to know about the student?"

I shake my head. They thank me and leave the office.

Next thing, word about Bradford's diary entry spreads around the campus. Most students believe it was the grades I'd given him earlier in the semester that led him to take his own life.

It's the second worst thing to being the prime suspect in a murder case.

CHAPTER 4

IT'S noon and I'm still glued to my office chair. Normally, I'm receiving emails from my students at this hour, asking me to explain their upcoming assignment, but not today. Bradford's death must have shaken everyone. The snow has built a layer big enough to cover the whole campus in white. I'm not a huge fan of Vermont winters, but I have no choice but to endure them. My wife, Emily, convinced me to stay and live in the state, and stay close to her family. I could have become a professor at Stanford, where the climate is warmer and more agreeable, but after long discussions with Emily right after we got married, I stuck around.

Perhaps I should have been more assertive in my negotiations.

An email from William comes through at twelve fifteen. He's calling for an emergency faculty meeting at three o'clock. The university canceled classes for the afternoon, so the students can seek professional help or bond with each other.

I stand up and feel a sharp pain in my hip. It still hurts from falling while skiing last winter. As I get older, bones heal much slower. I instinctively grab my hip and squeeze it hard. When I open my office door, our janitor, Danny, is cleaning the floor in the hallway. His head is bowed, and he jumps when he spots me.

"Hey, doc!"

I wonder if he knows I'm not an actual doctor, but a clinical psychologist with a PhD. It flatters me, and I don't mind. I consider myself a doctor of sorts.

Danny is an affable guy who has connected with a lot of students at the university. He stops whatever he's doing to check in with people. When he asks, 'how are you doing?' he means it. Students don't hesitate to open up to Danny's friendly face.

"Hey there." I say.

"How ya doing, doc?" he says. I see worry on his face.

"I'm fine." I answer as I walk past him. I don't care about exchanging niceties with him. Not today. I feel his eyes resting on my back before I hear the mop sweeping the floor again.

The cafeteria is almost empty. I order some noodle soup from the Asian cuisine. Carefully balancing the hot bowl in my hands, I walk straight to my office, avoiding eyes of people walking by.

At three, I head to the dean's conference room where

the faculty meeting is taking place. When I arrive, I'm hit with a heavy atmosphere. The room is large, with a long oval table and a plant in each corner of the room. Paintings of former university presidents have been hung on the walls. It's all men, but it doesn't strike me as unusual. At one end of the table sits William, greeting me with a quick nod. He's biting down his lip as he bows his head and stares down at his iPhone. His administrative assistant accompanies him to all his meetings to take minutes, but her absence is noticeable today.

I sit two chairs from William. As silence climbs up the walls, the room thickens with faculty members. Across from me sits a recently tenured literature professor. Her hair looks disheveled, and she's wearing a top with a large coffee stain. I narrow my eyes as I observe her. She is avoiding eye contact with everybody at the table and her eyes dart from object to object in the room. *What is she so agitated about?*

Twenty faculty members have gathered around the table, all awaiting William's words. He stores his phone in the blazer pockets and shoots a look at everyone. He nods at us, like we're his soldiers who just returned from a battle.

"Thank you for meeting with me on such a short notice." He clears his throat. He puts his hands on the table and sighs. "I presume you know why we are here. The unfortunate news of the student's passing has made the university reflect on our values as an institution. The deans had a long meeting with the president this morning and discussed the ramifications of the student's death."

Silence grows more uncomfortable. William looks around as if to study our faces, but he gets no cues from anyone.

"I understand we are here to educate our students. We are proud of that. You should be proud of that. But we are all responsible for our students' health and state of mind."

A slight commotion ensues in the room. Someone coughs. I twirl in my chair and stare at William, who's steadily growing nervous. He's rubbing the back of his neck as he clears his throat.

"What we had in mind is that we need to reevaluate the way we grade our students."

"Can you expand on that?" a male voice says on the other end of the table.

"Absolutely. We are considering implementing a grade inflation. I'm not saying you should give out all As, but we must adjust our standards to the new circumstances. We can't have students taking their lives because of a D or a C. Even though most students don't see it that way, there is more to life than college, and a poor grade shouldn't be followed with a punishment. Or a self-punishment in this case."

At this, my brows stitch together and anger rises inside me. I didn't study for decades in order to give As to lazy students. That won't happen as long as I am alive.

Besides, I'm feeling attacked as William shoots a gaze at me. I sit upright and look around the room. "If I may say something?"

"Of course."A slight smile forms on William's lips.

"I believe you are taking severe measures for a death of one student. We are here to pass on excellent education, not to babysit these kids. I cringe at the thought of giving good grades to mediocre students. How fair is that to the intelligent, hard-working ones? You are asking us to accept laziness, mediocrity, and foolishness."

Heat radiates from my body and my cheeks redden. William looks at me with his mouth ajar. He looks down, as if thinking of an appropriate response. William has been appointed the chair of the department and is determined to maintain his good name and harmony among faculty members. But it will take a lot of effort to make everyone happy this time.

Primarily me.

"I hear what you're saying, but keep in mind that the grade inflation is low on the scale of importance. What's important is that all of our students come out of the program alive. We don't want to risk a bad rep based on students killing themselves because of poor grades. I'd rather be cautious and lenient than imposing impossible requirements leading to students taking their life. Unfortunately, this is not up for a debate. The president has already decided and will send out a memo in a day or two."

The news shocks me like a strike to the jaw. Faculty input has been disregarded. This is humiliating.

"When's the grade inflation coming into effect?" someone asks.

"Most likely this coming spring."

Questions are pouring in from all sides, but I tune out. This entire premise of lowering our standards angers me. I can't hear anything from the thoughts lingering in my mind. I stand up, give William a quick look, and head for the door. The discussion has become heated, and I don't want to be a part of it.

CHAPTER 5

AFTER THE FACULTY MEETING, I go to my office and check my email one more time before I head home. The snow has sufficiently fallen down to cause havoc on the roads. My home is close to the university—a fifteen-minute ride by car. When Emily insisted we live in Vermont, I negotiated to be as close as possible to my workplace. Hers is not that far from the house, either. I hate driving. If I could walk to work every day, I'd be happier. But the roads are windy, and have no sidewalks, so they are not conducive to it.

When I arrive home, the house is empty. It's only three thirty in the afternoon, so that's not a surprise. Emily must be in her studio. Her business has grown so much over the past few years that she had to hire people to run it. She loves her job as a yoga and meditation teacher. Everybody loves her. Her mind is pure, and she's always light and positive. It's the reason I fell in love with her.

But lately, Emily and I have not been in sync. I can't put my finger on what the problem is, but I can sense she and I have grown apart as a couple. It could be that her role as a business owner has been all-consuming, and the pressure has become too much for her. Or, it could be that I've asked her several times if we can sit down and plan a family. We're not getting any younger. I'm approaching forty, and Emily is thirty-eight. No one can tell she's that old, but good looks don't matter to fertility.

Given the tension in our marriage, I decide to stay silent about Bradford's death. She doesn't need to find out, especially in light of the new perception on the campus that I am the one to blame for it.

Emily, as usual, will come home today and tell me all about her clients. Most of them become her friends, and I can no longer keep up with all of their names.

The house feels dead without her cheer.

It's also cold, so I turn up the heat to seventy. I rub my palms together, then blow into them for heat. The base-boards crackle as the heat pumps up. My jacket is still on, and I hesitate to take it off until the house warms up a bit. In the kitchen, I open the bar and pour myself half a glass of whiskey. I add a little ice, but not too much to not dilute the alcohol.

I'm ruminating over my day, still angry about our faculty meeting. The whiskey takes away my anger, and I focus on what's happening right now. I sit in the recliner and put on Netflix. It's usually Emily who's home first from work, so I'm disoriented. And maybe lonely. The house is creepy when it's so quiet and empty. As I scroll down the movie menu, I get a text from Emily to tell me the road conditions are horrible and to be careful.

She is so caring. Despite the tension as of late, she remains kind toward me, which makes me weary. I'd rather her blow up at me and express all her feelings rather than tactfully avoid it by being cordial and pleasant all the time.

Because I know that bad shit has crawled under her skin, hiding something underneath.

Her message still makes me smile, but I don't respond. It will be a fun surprise that I'm already home when she arrives.

Twenty minutes later, the front door opens. Her voice echoes and reaches me from the foyer. "Mitch!"

She must have seen my car parked out front.

"Mitch, you're home already?" She's now standing in the living room, and her face looks bewildered. "Should I be happy or worried about that?"

I laugh. "It's all good. You should be happy."

I jump out of the recliner and give her a kiss. She opens up her arms and takes me into her embrace. After a slight hug, she moves away and narrows her eyes at me. "Are you drinking?"

"Yeah." I say. "Just one to take the edge off."

"Why? Is everything okay?" Worry covers her face.

"Yes. Everything's fine. Just work stuff."

I don't tell Emily about Bradford dying. I don't share about the faculty meeting. She'd be a brilliant listener, but I don't let my problems fester or affect our already-strained marriage. Emily and I don't fight about big stuff, which is what concerns me. The shallowness of our relationship will only cause the distance between us to grow. We always compromise and embrace the middle ground, with neither one feeling satisfied.

She walks to the kitchen and yells out about dinner. She wants to know what I want to eat, my least favorite question.

"Oh, I don't know." I call back. "Pick whatever."

I hear the dishes rattling in the kitchen while I watch a movie picked at random. My attention bounces between the screen and the events of today. I take a sip of the whiskey and deeply inhale. Emily comes back to the living room to tell me the food will be ready soon. She kisses me on the forehead. "What's my handsome husband watching?"

"Some random movie."

She gazes at the TV screen and back at me, smiling. "Maybe we can watch a movie in bed after the dinner." She winks at me and smiles. Emily likes to refer to sex as a movie.

I smile back. It's something we've avoided for a while, as one of us always seems to have an excuse. If my memory serves me well, it's been several weeks since we made love.

Emily is quite generous with pleasing me in bed. It's one thing that stood out when we first started dating. A pure mind with dirty deeds. But I loved her more for it.

"Sure." I say.

As she turns her back to me and walks away, she tells me the dinner will be ready in ten minutes.

While we're eating, Emily gives me a sly look. I wonder what she's thinking about, but I know she'll eventually come out and tell me. For now, I don't ask.

"How do you like the burrito?"

"It's good," I say.

"Glad you like it," she says. Her eyes don't shift from me as she takes a bite of her burrito. When she finishes chewing up a bite, she stands up to open up a bottle of red wine. Over her shoulder, she asks me if I want a glass.

"No, thanks. I'll have another whiskey."

She goes to the living room to retrieve my whiskey glass and pours another.

"Today was slow at the studio. A bunch of people didn't show up because of the snow."

"Oh."

"Winters are usually slower, so I'll need to up my marketing plan."

"Sounds good."

"Thank God my staff is hard-working. Miguel is brilliant at what he does."

Miguel is her right hand and he does whatever Emily asks him to do. He'd do anything to show genuine compassion and loyalty to the studio. I've grown tired of her bragging about him all the time. But I say nothing. I don't want Emily to think I am jealous. Well, I may be a little jealous, but she doesn't need to know that.

I look up from my burrito and see Emily beaming. I nod at her and say it's good she can trust him.

"Hey, babe." Her tone shifts, and I know something more serious is about to come out of her mouth. "Maybe tonight isn't the best time to bring up this subject, but I want us to talk about something that's been on my mind lately."

My eyes widen as I stare at her. "Umm?"

She takes another sip of her wine. Her throat moves as she swallows, and I observe each little movement.

"I think I'm ready for us to plan a family." She nods quickly and offers a tentative smile.

"Oh." I don't expect her to bring up this subject. "Well—"

"You know what?" She pitches her voice. "How about I take you out for dinner this week, and we talk about it then?"

"Sure." I say. I appreciate her suggestion, because I'm not in the mood to discuss the matter of growing our family on the day like this. But I'm glad she's finally come around. I desperately want kids. I just can't bring myself to talk about that tonight.

"Cool."

After dinner, we head to the bedroom. She turns on Netflix and puts on *Breakfast at Tiffany's*. My eyelids are closing, and I can't seem to keep them open. Twenty minutes into the movie, Emily lies on top of me and gently plants kisses all over my body. But I'm too buzzed from alcohol to feel a desire to make love. I nuzzle Emily to the side, mumbling something, before turning around and falling asleep.

THURSDAY

THE SNOW STOPPED ACCUMULATING by the morning. Snowplows had worked at clearing the streets all night. The roads are now clear of snow and ice, but they're full of salt, so I need to get my car washed soon. I head to work early, as I need to work on submitting my article for publication. Teaching and researching are my duties as a professor. My research subjects are part of a major hospital nearby, and I visit the hospital regularly to meet with them and interpret my research.

My field of study is focused on how trauma and PTSD influence the human brain. It addresses mainly a psychological side. My human subjects are an array of people with deeply rooted issues. I've come across ex-soldiers who've experienced the death of their comrades in battle on a daily basis. I've encountered women who have suffered violence at the hands of their husbands. I've worked with children who weren't shown love and affection by their parents. I've studied those who've had near-death experiences, and their trauma has resulted in their journey of survival.

I can't say their stories haven't affected me, but if I break down, my research would no longer be objective. Which it must be to maintain my credibility among the scholars in the field. I need to be the best.

My article is close to being finished. As I drive, I reflect on what needs to be done to finalize the draft. When I arrive at the campus, it's eerily quiet. It's still early for any life to be visible on the outside. The snow has melted on the path, and snow patches are still lingering here and there.

Before I focus on the article, I check my email. One from William. An exclamation point on the top says it's urgent. He must be unhappy that I abruptly left the faculty meeting yesterday. I open his email, and sure enough, he wants to meet with me this morning. One on one. I hit reply and write: *Sure. I'll come by your office at eleven.*

I close my email and get back to my article. This one will lead to many citations, as it's groundbreaking. I know that getting it published in *Nature* is extremely competitive, but this article deserves nothing but.

Even though my office door is closed, I can hear the whistling echoing along the hallway, and it sounds like a hollow cry. I cringe. I launch out of the chair and head for the door. When I open it, I see Danny, the janitor, standing nearby and sweeping the floors. I'm standing right there, but he acts like I'm not, and just keeps wiping the floors while creating a lot of noise.

I clear my throat. "Excuse me."

He flinches and stops sweeping, looking up at me. His hand goes up in the air and he waves. "Hey, doc!" His lips form into a big smile. He is always so cheerful and positive. It's almost annoying.

"Hey. If you don't mind—" I place my index finger on my lips, but he looks puzzled.

"Yes, doc?" He places his palms on the broom top and watches me with intense eyes.

"The whistling. Can you stop? I can't concentrate."

He perks up. "Oh. Of course, doc. No worries."

He waves at me and picks up the sweeping. I nod and enter my office. Silence comes again. The deadline is fast approaching so I hurry to edit the article.

I've lost track of time when someone knocks on my door. I peek at the clock. Almost ten. I don't invite the person in when the door opens up. It's Sarah. She's my teaching assistant and a bright and zealous PhD student. Sarah should graduate this coming spring. It has taken her only five years to do her PhD, a record time.

Ever since she got into the program, she's been reminding me that her aspiration is to be a chief clinical psychologist in the top U.S. hospital. She has pestered me to keep that in mind and, when the time comes, to give her a recommendation or somehow provide her a gateway to her desired career. She knows I have a lot of contacts that can help her get a jumpstart as soon as she finishes her studies.

"Hey, Mitch," she says.

I smirk. "I've asked you many times not to call me that."

"Oh, sorry." She puts a sly smile on. "Professor Wegner." She throws a bunch of blue booklets on my desk and says, "I'm done grading the midterms."

She looks at me evenly, and I can't tell if the results are any good. I always hope my students take a considerable amount of time to immerse themselves in the subject and learn something valuable.

Sarah slumps in the chair across from me. She crosses her leg and looks at me with sultry eyes. "Can you guess the average?"

"I ... I ..." I stutter and shake my head. "I don't know. Tell me!"

"B plus."

A sense of relief washes over me. It's not as bad as I thought.

"Okay," I say. "I will hand these out in class today."

I grab the booklets and square them together against the tabletop. Sarah is staring at me, motionless, as if she wants to say something.

"Yes?" I invite her.

"Nothing. I better get going." She stands up, then says. "Bradford's exam is in there, too. A straight A. Look at it."

Sarah turns around and leaves my office. I plow through the exams and find the one that belongs to Bradford. His cursive handwriting is easy to spot. But there's something strange about his exam. Something doesn't seem right.

It's killing me. I can't figure it out.

I flip the pages and read his responses. They are thorough and descriptive. It gives me goosebumps. It's obvious he studied hard for this. If he was certain he would do well and correct his grades, why would he kill himself? Something is fishy about all this.

When I get to the last page, his writing becomes wobblier and rackety. It's almost like someone else wrote it. I keep flipping the pages until I get to the very last one.

The blood freezes in my veins when I see the image on the last page.

It's a drawing of a knife with blood oozing from it. My chest tightens and the room feels too hot. Has Sarah done this to mess with me? I can see her doing something like this. She has drawn strange things on exam booklets in the past. Out of boredom, she'd said.

But what if she didn't?

What if Bradford drew it and wanted to communicate something with me? Maybe I should show this to Officer Banks, in case he can make better sense of it than I can.

I open up the bottom draw of my desk and shove the exam beneath the pile of books and papers. I won't tell anyone about it. No one is ever going to see it.

I also won't tell anyone that Bradford and I had a brief, intense exchange in my office not long ago. He'd knocked hard on my office, visibly upset, and stormed in like he was escaping from someone or something chasing him.

As soon as he stepped inside, he told me his father would never forgive him if his GPA dropped. By the end of his monologue, tears were streaming down his face. I watched him and wondered what number his parents had done on him to cause him to behave in such a cowardly way. Instead of reassuring him that everything would turn out okay, I told him to pull himself together and study harder. He stood in the middle of my office with his clenched fists, his eyes narrowing at me, telling me through gritted teeth that I would regret saying that. He'd stormed out of my office and slammed the door behind him.

That was the last time I saw Bradford. Two days later, he was dead.

A thought suddenly occurs to me as I am reflecting on our last exchange.

Bradford's diary.

The realization smacks me like a boxing glove. The writings on the exam and in his diary appear to be so different, leading to many questions. How is it possible the writings belong to the same person? Did the police confirm the diary was Bradford's?

I can't help but think that something sinister is at play.

CHAPTER 7

AT ELEVEN, I head to William's office. It's been a while since I was there. He and I have had mainly a cordial and professional working relationship since I joined the university. He has been a champion of my research and has supported me all along. But today is different. I don't think William invited me to exchange niceties or to discuss my research. There's no doubt he has something important to tell me, and my guess is that it's related to yesterday's faculty meeting.

I knock on his office door and push it open. William is at his desk, his glasses off. I do a double take, as he looks almost unrecognizable without them. I don't think I've ever seen him without them. Now that I'm right in front of him, it's his angry expression that's making me uneasy.

We greet each other with a nod and say nothing. He extends his arm toward a chair in the room and tells me to sit. His office looks different since I last saw it—the walls look painted in a lighted color and the furniture looks like an upgrade from the old desk he used to have. The office smells fresh and inviting. My eyes dart towards all his diplomas hanging on the wall behind him. He's been so proud of his Yale degree. It's a focal point in a large frame, like his most prized possession.

I sit down and look at William. His eyes have dark circles, and his hair is greasy and disheveled. I've never seen such a display from him before. My guess is he intends to give me a long-winded scolding about the way I spoke in the faculty meeting yesterday, but I'm ready for the onslaught. When I know I'm making the right choices, I'm in a state of serenity. No one can shake my belief system.

"I'm very unhappy with how things went in our meeting yesterday," he says. His voice is deeper and louder than usual. As I suspected, no niceties. William's the type of person who will always inquire about your weekend, your wife's wellbeing, and if you have any vacation plans coming up, but not now.

"For you to protest so openly is a disgrace," he continues. "The least you could do is stay through the meeting and learn about others' opinions on the situation."

I tilt my head and narrow my eyes. "What should I care about others' opinions, William? I have opinions of my own."

He slams his palm on the desk and raises his voice by a few decibels. I sit up straighter in the chair and open my eyes wider. "You see, that's your problem, Mitch. You don't give a damn about other people. Success doesn't lie in how many articles you have published, or how many citations you have garnered. Ultimately, it's about people and how we treat them."

His face reddens, and his spittle almost reaches me.

"Have I mistreated someone?" My voice is calm, and I think it's making William angrier.

"You don't walk out on a meeting like you did yesterday. Show some respect for your colleagues and this institution."

I smirk. "I've given a lot to this institution by mainly upholding its reputation. I'm the best in my field, and the institution should be proud to have someone like me."

"Listen, I have always admired you and your aptitude for excellence. I'm aware you are one of the best in your field, and I won't argue with that. But this is not the time to boast about high standards, and definitely not the time to pursue them. We just lost a student because of grades, Mitch. We cannot let that happen ever again. Do you understand me?"

His voice is so whiny, and it doesn't match the William I'm familiar with. I shake my head. "I can't bring myself to belittle the years of hard work I've put in, William. You can't make me."

"You are pathetic," he says through his teeth.

"Oh."

"Today, the president is sending out a memo to

faculty about the grade inflation. The policy is going into effect in the spring. You will have time to reconcile and go along with it." He narrows his eyes at me and taps his fingers on the chair armrest, as if he's expecting a wild reaction from me. We stare at each other for a few intense seconds. A cunning grin takes over my face.

"Listen, William." I say. "I am not here to argue with you. I hear your concerns, and I will take them into consideration." (I won't). "Now, if you excuse me, I need to prepare for my class."

There's no sense in debating him any further. What's done is done. The university is taking it in the direction I disagree with, and my opinion doesn't seem to matter.

I stand up to leave his office. As I walk through the door, I can feel the weight of William's menacing eyes on my back. We've never had an intense and confrontational discussion until today. I fear it might not be our last. I ponder on whether my sound position on the matter will alter his view of me.

The hallway is ghostly, except for a few students trying to get to their class. Judging by their speed, it appears they're running late.

By the time I get to my office, the email from the president about grade inflation has already arrived. He is also urging us to help the students to look for help through free university counseling and the hotline I established—if we ever witness them in a state of anxiety. A separate email with such content will go out to the students soon.

Another email arrives from William, calling for another faculty meeting today at four. It doesn't say what it's about. But we're all expected to show up.

I close my computer and head for the door to teach class.

CHAPTER 8

THE FIRST THING I see when I walk into the amphitheater-style classroom is that the front rows are empty. The students have congregated in the last rows, as far from the front as possible. Most of them are staring at their phones and some are reading from the textbooks. I put the exam booklets on the desk and gaze at the students. No one is looking at me or paying me any attention. Their faces are sullen and disinterested. They aren't usually this quiet. The classroom is usually filled with whispers, phone notifications, and the rustling of pages.

The cause of distress is obviously Bradford's death. The students also have learned about his diary and rumors are circling that it's all my fault that he took his own life. I want to debunk their belief, and I prepare a little speech in my head.

Bradford's death has been the main talking point at the university. We'd learned this morning that Bradford's autopsy result revealed he died of cyanide poisoning. No one knows how he got ahold of the substance, but everyone assumes he broke into the chemistry lab and stole it. Then he went to his dorm room and took the poison. It's an instant death sentence. Once you take it, even in small doses, your body convulses, then your mouth fills with a mixture of saliva, blood and vomit. You pass out, and then you die. A body is deprived of oxygen completely.

But the dying part is quick. Only twenty minutes.

As soon as the coroner delivered the autopsy results, Officer Banks returned to the university and checked out the chemistry lab. He couldn't uncover any evidence of an intrusion, but, after conversing with the lab manager, he deduced a bottle of cyanide had been removed from the locked shelf. He and Officer Moy interviewed every faculty member with past and present access to the lab, and all of them had appeared bewildered by the news. All had a strong alibi—which will be fortunate for them if Bradford's death is deemed a murder.

The detectives had visited Bradford's dorm and turned it upside down, searching for the bottle. They couldn't find any evidence that Bradford stole it. It was entirely possible he took it outside the dorm, disposed of the bottle, and returned to his room, where he died.

Above his desk, while reading a textbook.

His classmates look unsettled. I get a sense they'd want to talk about it if I started the conversation. But no one says a word. It's going to be hard to engage them. They must be wondering if taking one's life over studies is truly worth it. A young, happy-go-lucky fellow is gone. Bradford was a type of person who was determined to excel in life. He was the glue in the community. His death is a gap filled with wounds. What are the students going to do without him?

I don't address any of it with the students. Not yet. I shall let them ruminate until they're comfortable raising the subject. I turn my focus to the exams, and I read the names from the booklets, asking the students to raise their hand. I walk up to them and hand them their exam. We do this in dead silence. The students who received less than a B don't look shaken or upset. They flip through the pages, close the booklet, and store it inside the textbook.

The atmosphere is chilling and borderline uncomfortable.

When I've finished handing out their exams, I ask if anyone has questions about their grades.

Crickets.

"Well, if no one has questions or worries about their grade, we can move on and address a new topic of the week: post-traumatic stress disorder."

I turn around to the writing board and my hand draws automatically for the chalk. I write on the board: PTSD. While I'm still facing the board, a voice behind me draws my immediate attention.

"Why did you kill Bradford?"

Every molecule within me goes still. It's a voice I don't recognize. My arm drops from the writing position, and it hangs along my side. The sudden blankness of my mind leaves space for the anger that's rising up inside, and as it fills it, the fury spills out onto my reddening cheeks. I hold my breath, blinking a little longer than normal. Then I swallow down the rage and force my body into a reluctant state of calmness.

I turn slowly and dart my eyes around the room. Everyone has a poker face. I try to locate the source, but I can't tell where the voice came from.

I look at Nick, an A student in the far-left corner, and he's staring back at me. His expression is not giving away any clues. He has admired me since day one, and I'd hope he'd back me up. But Nick is frozen in place.

My eyes move to the other students. They look somewhat proud and dignified. For a second, I question myself. Had I misheard or imagined the words? But I'm pretty sure I heard the question loud and clear.

"Who said that?" I ask. My voice is calm, but inside, I'm fuming.

Silence permeates the room again.

If this was a Bradford vs Mitch sparring match, I'd be bleeding dead now.

I raise my voice and ask again, "Who said that?"

But frozen faces stare at me. Someone lets out a chuckle. My head jerks toward the sound, but I can't decipher who it was.

They all think I am the reason Bradford took his own life. It's a herd mentality. It only takes one person to start a belief, and then everyone else follows suit, like a cult.

That thought gets me angrier. I must be in charge of the situation.

"Everyone, grab a piece of paper from your notebook. I'm giving you an impromptu quiz."

The students look around with raised eyebrows. Someone in the back cusses me out. But I'm so riled up that I pay little attention.

"In a free essay style, I want you to write a definition of post-traumatic disorder, the effects on people, and describe one example given in the textbook." I look at my watch. "You have thirty minutes."

This will teach them a lesson. Possibly it won't, but at least for the moment, I'll feel like I'm in control.

Silent commotion occurs in the room. No one is talking, but they're looking at each other, nodding, and smiling.

I take my phone out of my pocket and notice a text from Emily. She likes to contact me between her sessions and brag about how divine everybody in the class felt. I don't respond and choose to read the news instead.

There's nothing in the local news about Bradford dying. The university has disallowed the local stations to report on the campus. Since it's a private campus, the university has the choice of either involving the FBI or opting for a private investigation. Unlike the last time, when a student took her life, and the whole town knew about it, Bradford's death seems more of a taboo than anything. But this gives me great relief, because the chances of Emily finding out are slim to none.

The news on the campus spread like a wildfire, but it will most likely stay there.

I look at my watch. Half an hour has passed. I tell everyone to stop writing and hand in their quiz.

"Don't forget to put down your name." I instruct them to take a ten-minute break and put their quiz on my desk.

One by one, they march toward me like soldiers. Their expressions seem lighter. I'm glad they didn't mind me giving them an impromptu quiz. But I must remain the authority in the classroom. They need to know who they are dealing with.

Within seconds, the classroom is empty.

I look up at the seats, and they are void of any objects —no jackets, no textbooks, nothing. Have they all left without returning?

A strange suspicion gnaws at me. I feel like someone or something is watching me, and I look around to find the culprit. But I'm all alone, standing in front of the desk, wondering what has just happened.

The pieces of paper on my desk draw my eyes. I approach them and pick up one. I turn it around, and my eyes widen at the shocking scribble that has me nearly choked.

In big letters, I read: *You're an asshole.*

I place it back on the desk and pick up another one: *Did you know you're a psychopath Hahaha.*

I imagine a sinister laugh in my head.

Then the next one: *I think you should teach at another university ... douche.*

A frown spreads across my face and my jaw twitches. I want to pick up another quiz, but I refuse to subject myself to this abuse.

As I sift through the papers quickly, I notice none of them have a name on. I guess they call this some kind of protest.

But I call it a war.

CHAPTER 9

I DON'T FEEL like attending the faculty meeting, but I decide to go anyway. I stroll down to the dean's conference room and enter hesitantly. The faculty sitting at the table look preoccupied, their eyes engrossed in something in front of them. William is sitting in the same spot he sat in yesterday. He's reading from his iPad and doesn't flinch when I sit next to him. In fact, I think he's ignoring me intentionally. I sulk at his gesture, but I don't let him notice it.

When everyone seems to be present, William starts off by saying we are all here because he wants to give us updates related to Bradford's death. The news here spreads like wildfire, so I'm sure everyone already knows what he is about to say.

"Bradford died of cyanide poisoning." He dives right in. "The police have ruled out a murder and believe it is suicide."

I feel eyes peeled on me. I straighten out in my chair and lift my head high. No words come out of my mouth. I suspect William will go into the grade inflation charade, and before I finish that thought, he's already on the topic. His eyes gaze at me as if he means to convey this message to me only. Everyone else nods in approval without seeming to have any questions or concerns. I gaze back at William and give him a small smile.

The meeting is adjourned after fifteen minutes. We all stand up in unison and walk out in silence. On my way to the office, I see Sarah with a student. They're sitting at a table, and she looks animated, gesturing with her arms and explaining something. When she sees me, she stops for a second, gives me a wave, and winks. I turn my head and pretend I hadn't noticed her. She must realize winking at me is highly inappropriate, but I must admit it turns me on.

I still wonder if she's the one who drew the knife and the blood in Bradford's exam booklet. Does she know something? If she did, I wonder what she knows and what her motive behind doing it is.

On my way to the office, I see Danny. He stops what he's doing and smiles at me. "Hey, doc. Sorry about whistling. I won't do it again."

I raise my hand and wave it at him. "No worries." My eyebrows are furrowed. I feel it, but I'm happy he is acknowledging his misbehavior. Sometimes I wish I could be as easygoing as him, but I imagine his daily burden is not the same as mine. All he does is wipe floors and make sure the classrooms are clean, sanitized, and neat.

Me? I'm saving the world. One person at a time.

The students have left me bewildered with their remarks on the exam today. I'm in no mood to hang around the campus any longer. I can finish the article in the comfort of my home, with an iced glass of whiskey next to me. I close my computer and exit my office, locking it behind me. The only other person who has keys to my office is Danny—he has the master key and unlocks every door in the evening to empty the trash bins. It's a tedious task, but that's what he does every day, whether the trash bins are full. The other person who has a key to my office is our master administrator. She never comes around and occasionally sends emails to the faculty, informing them of new administrative policies we should know. Her name is Rebecca Wilson, and I don't know what she looks like. I have never seen her.

Bradford's exam is safely locked in the desk drawer. I don't suppose anyone in their right mind would think of deliberately opening it and looking for suspicious evidence.

In the parking lot, I find my car looking filthy from the mud and salt the snow had brought the night earlier.

I run my hand over my hair and decide it is time for a haircut. I like to keep up my dashing looks. A new haircut gives me more confidence. I decide to go to my usual barbershop around the corner from my house. The barber, Henry, who I usually see, has been there forever. He knows me by name and likes to chat me up whenever I go see him.

On my way there, the town looks ghostly and gray. Only a few people walk down the street, shielding themselves from the cold under multiple layers. I hate how October turns into the ice age in Vermont. It's way too soon to hunker down at home and wait for spring days to cheer me up. We're inching closer to daylight savings time, when four o'clock will bring darkness.

On my way to the barbershop, I stop by the carwash on the corner of Main and Elm Street. A few cars are lined up in front of me, but it goes relatively fast. When my turn comes, the man in a uniform asks me what type of wash I want. I tell him I want the whole works: the most expensive deal. Upon entering the washing garage, the foam coats the windshield, and the brush, resembling long spaghetti, goes back and forth, eliminating the dirt from the car. I wish I could wipe away the negative things the students have said about me in the same manner.

The car wash belt spits out my car minutes later, and I turn to the left and head to the barbershop.

When I pull up to the barbershop, the foggy windows make me question if it's open. But Henry is almost never closed. He's owned the barbershop for decades and has closed the shop only once, when he'd had had a heart attack. He was taken to the hospital where he stayed and quickly recovered in a few days. His goal was to return to the only refuge that sustained him: his shop and the loyal customers who he'd served for years. When I get closer, I see the shop is open. I enter and Henry greets me like I'm his best friend. His voice is cheerful, albeit his body frame frail and old. To be a good barber, he knows that being entertaining and interested in people is part of the deal. Many customers a lot older than himself keep coming back for a cut and his company.

"Mitch!"

"Hey, Henry." I smile, but my gesture feels tired and disingenuous.

"I haven't seen you in a while. Take a seat." He points his hand at a chair and tells me he would be with me shortly. In front of him is a man in his forties who looks a lot like Henry. "Mitch, this is my son, Drew. He came to visit for a few days."

I don't care about his son or his visit, but I offer another smile and a wave in the mirror, where our eyes meet. "Mitch."

"Hey, Mitch," Drew says. His voice is deep and authoritative.

"Drew moved to Florida recently for a job," Henry continues. "I'm grateful he still comes to visit." He stops what he is doing and taps his son on the shoulder. "So, what's new with you, Mitch?"

"Absolutely nothing." I usually appreciate Henry's

inquiry, but not today. I usually tell him what I've been working on lately and how my students are doing, but today, I've got nothing for him.

Henry glances in the mirror once in a while to catch my gaze. "And how's your wife?"

"Good." I'm short with him and hope this will stop him from asking me further questions.

"How's teaching?"

"Teaching?" I find my heart rate increase at this question, and I feel half-guilty that I'm about to lie. "Excellent. The students seem to enjoy my class."

Henry is doing the last touch-ups on his son's hair when he turns to me and says, "You don't know about the suicide that happened recently, do you?"

I freeze. I hate being questioned about something I've been hiding from my wife, and I certainly don't want the news to circle around the town. I wonder how Henry found out, but it may not be a big surprise given his profession. It's quite possible a student came to visit him. I just hope the student wasn't mine.

"I know little about it. The university officials prefer we do not discuss the case."

"I understand." Henry continues finishing the job.

I look at my watch and sudden unease flows through my body. I fidget in my seat and my skin starts to crawl as if thousands of worms are climbing up from my feet to my head. To escape them, I jump on my feet and tell Henry I have to go. I'll be back.

I ignore Henry when he tells me to wait until he's done with his son. The little bell on the door dingles as I open it, and I run to my car, eager to get home and have a drink.

CHAPTER 10

EMILY IS at home when I arrive. Her car has taken up more space than necessary at the front of our house. I sneak in and park next to her car, irritated by her carelessness. I've told her several times already to be careful and not take too much space, and she does it again. Does she ever listen?

I enter the house, and classical music is playing through the house speakers. I'm not really in the mood for music, but I still pause to observe that it's Mozart's *Magic Flute* she's playing. Emily seems to appreciate all music genres, but she's the only woman I have been with who appreciates classical music. Her love for diverse arts and culture made her stand out from all the other women I used to date. But as time goes on, my excitement about who my wife is has waned. Time does that—it changes our perspective on things and people.

When I slam the front door, she comes behind the kitchen wall, holding a glass of red wine.

"Oh, hi, honey." She greets me with a huge smile and comes to me for a kiss. She plants one on my right cheek, but I don't reciprocate.

"Hey," I say.

"How was your day?" She seems over-the-top cheerful and I'm curious to know what has driven her to this state.

"Okay." I'm short. I walk to the kitchen and open up the fridge to see what's there to eat. It's almost empty except for eggs, a milk cardboard, a two-litter soda bottle, and leftover Indian food from the other night. The sink is filled with dishes that seem to have accumulated over the past week. I cringe at the sight and wonder what she's been up to.

My eyebrows draw together as I glance quickly at her, sitting at the kitchen table with her phone in her hands and a smile on her face. Yoga pants and a tight T-shirt— her work attire—are still on her. Her body is in perfect shape, not an ounce of fat is showing, and sometimes I envy her profession. I wish I had time for a gym or yoga. I'm not fat, by any means, but I'm not muscular either. I definitely could use some exercise.

I sit opposite her, and she puts her phone on the table and looks up at me.

"Emma's just told me Brian popped the question to her last night. How exciting is that? Apparently, he put the ring in her drink when they went to a bar, and she almost swallowed it." Emily's laughing loudly, and her laughter is usually contagious. I don't laugh back, because I find the proposal dumb and juvenile. "Anyway, they want us to have dinner tomorrow night. I'd really like you to come."

Emily well knows I'm not a social type. In fact, I don't have a lot of friends remaining and I tend to socialize with her friends only on special occasions. Marriage proposals, weddings, births, BBQs and such. I've met Emma several times. She is Emily's best friend from high school, and they've kept a close relationship since. I find her obnoxious with her high-pitched voice and overly made-up face. And her fiancé, Brian? He's got to be the biggest meathead I've met. He's one of those people I have nothing personal against, but he just rubs me the wrong way. Despite the dreadful thought of getting together with the couple, I don't want to disappoint my wife.

"Sure," I declare.

"Great!" she says. "I'll let her know."

Emily stands up from the chair and exits the kitchen. As I stare at the table, I picture smashing Brian's face against it with my fist. I question what's gotten into me. Why am I finding pleasure in imagining decapitating Brian's mug? I surmise the whole situation at work has stirred up rage inside me, and I can't let go. It's like a big black cloud hanging over my head and the rain pours over me with a vengeance.

Emily's phone lights up, and it draws my immediate

attention. She's gotten a text from someone. I am assuming it's from Emma to let her know where and what time to meet them tomorrow, but I'm taken aback when I see his name instead. It's Miguel, her "right hand" as she calls him.

I lean forward to catch the entirety of his message and tap on the phone once to see the message closely.

Don't tell our secret to anyone.

There's a wink and a hug emoji accompanying those words. My face contorts and my body tenses up.

What hidden information is Miguel referring to? Is Emily cheating on me with this dud? What's going on here? It could be that Emily is so happy, not because Emma got engaged, but because her secret with Miguel makes her feel unique, wanted, and cherished? Many thoughts run through my mind. Is this why Emily and I have grown distanced in the recent past? It all makes sense now why she no longer calls me her favorite teddy bear, or why she no longer has the kind of admiration and respect she showed me at the beginning of our marriage.

I'm confused and shake my head as I reconcile this new reality—if that's what this is.

I'm scared of what this means, but I will let her tell me of her own volition. I'm sure his text is innocent.

Emily returns to the kitchen, mid-sentence, talking about a client she met today. I attempt to listen, but Miguel's text flashes in front of my eyes. She sits at the table, grabs her phone, skims the message, and puts it back down. Her eyes meet mine, but her countenance remains expressionless. She doesn't smile, doesn't give any clues whether the message she just read has any effect on her.

"What do you feel like for dinner?" she asks.

I'm expecting her to tell me what Miguel has said in his text—and what he means—but a nauseating feeling tells me she won't be addressing it at all.

Who is Emily? What is she hiding?

I tell her I am not hungry and head to the bar to pour myself a glass of whiskey. She's still sitting at the kitchen table and giggling. I try to avoid her joy—I hurry into my office and close the door with a bang.

FRIDAY

WHEN I WAKE UP, one thing is different than usual: I'm not sleeping in the same bed as my wife. I'm lying on my office couch alone, crunched up, in pain from sleeping in an uncomfortable position all night. My memory from last night is foggy, except that I had a copious amount of whiskey. I must have blacked out at some point and found my way to the couch.

But something else immediately occurs to me. Emily never came to my rescue like she usually does when I fall asleep in my office. Or maybe she did, but I couldn't hear her. I look at my alarm clock sitting on my desk and see it's past eight. Emily must have already gone to her studio. She gets there early so she can take care of everything else before she teaches lessons.

But I wonder now if she has a different motive. I wonder if she and Miguel spend time together, and giggle and daydream about what their life together could be.

I prop myself up on the couch and instinctually grab my throbbing head. The whiskey aftertaste is still lingering in my mouth. The smell is permeated in my pores. I open the office door and look to my left and right, as if I'm hiding from someone, and I listen to sounds. But it's dead quiet. As I walk to the kitchen, I slam into a dining chair and curse under my breath.

The morning energy is giving me a bad vibe, as if something horrendous is going to happen.

In the kitchen, I push the start button on the coffeemaker, and the saving grace in the form of coffee almost instantly begins to drip into the carafe. I open up the kitchen cabinet to retrieve the biggest mug, but as I reach for it, it slips out of my hand, falls on the floor, and smashes into hundreds of pieces.

I stand above the broken mug, staring at the debris. My first instinct is to ignore it and pick up another mug from the cabinet. But the better side of me tells me I should pick up the broken pieces before they hurt my feet.

People think breaking dishes is a sign of good luck. But I know better than that. Breaking dishes means there's negative energy inside me that's manifesting itself in carelessly smashing things. It's no surprise. The students are blaming me for Bradford's death, my wife might be cheating on me, and William has been unkind. It's time for me to seize control of my life.

For now, I need to clean up the mess in front of me.

I can't remember where Emily left the broom and the

dustpan. In all frankness, I don't know where most of the things in the house are located, since Emily is the one in our household that fixes things. While together, I don't think I have ever done the laundry or cleaned the house.

My head turns around like a dog trying to catch his own tail, looking for the cleaning tools. It occurs to me that the broom and dustpan are most likely down in the basement, where I once discovered accidentally that all our tools are kept.

The basement is located off the kitchen. Its stairways are deep, dark, and uninviting. They look similar to those in horror movies, but I never see it that way, since it's the house I live in, I own, and pay a mortgage for. When we looked for houses, Emily insisted upon buying one with historic quaint and charm. Our house was built in the nineteenth century, which is considered quite ancient in the area. With the historic charm also come several inconveniences, such as the neighboring houses being too close to our house or this basement. Next to us lives an old man who surveys us carefully, but we don't mind.

We keep the basement door closed all the time, because its descent from the kitchen is sudden, like a steep cliff hanging over the tumorous ocean.

I open the basement door, and the darkness startles me. The moldy scent serves as a reminder of how dreary the space feels.

I flip the light switch on my right and trudge down to the basement. The lightbulb buzzes and the furnace in the far corner of the basement kicks in, overriding the sound. At the bottom of the stairs is a narrow bearing wall, one step away from the stairway. It's placed there awkwardly, and I remember how hard it was to move large items into the basement and go around the wall when we first moved in.

In the corner of my eye, I see a cardboard box with my name written on it. The cardboard looks saggy from the many moldy nights spent here. I approach it, wondering what's inside. As I lift the lid, a musty smell wafts up, making me wrinkle my nose. Inside, I find an old photo album, its pages yellowed and faded with age.

My heart skips a beat as I see my mother and father smiling up at me from the first page. They look so young and carefree in the photo. But in the photo on the next page, I notice something strange. My father's face has been scribbled over with a black marker, so that all you can see is a dark blotch where his features would be.

Confused, I turn the page. There are more photos of my parents, but again, my father's face is blacked out in every single one. I don't understand why anyone would do such a thing, or who has done it.

As I continue flipping through the album, I notice something even more unsettling. In every photo, my mother looks sad, even when she's smiling. Her eyes look as if she is carrying a heavy burden.

Unease filling me, I rummage through the box, hoping to find some answers. As I sort through old school projects, I suddenly spot a manila envelope at the bottom. My heart racing, I pull it out and see it's labeled with my name and the words "Middle School." I recognize my mother's writing. Plus, she was the one who always organized things and kept them intact—well, except for her marriage.

My hands shake as I tear open the envelope and pear inside.

What I see makes my blood run cold. Stacks of paper, including old report cards, progress reports, and disciplinary records. I flip through the pages, feeling sick to my stomach as I see my name scrawled across numerous suspension notices. As I look at the dates on the papers, I realize the suspensions had started shortly after my father disappeared. Or left us. I never learned which exactly.

I've always thought my middle school years are a blur. Not even a faint memory has remained. My father's sudden disappearance has clouded all other recollections, and my mother and I being left alone is the only thing etched deeply into my subconscious.

Now it seems like the suspension notices are something far more sinister. A mystery of sorts.

I'm confused by this discovery. There's obviously something dark and twisted lurking in my past. But now is not the time to dig.

As I put the box in its place, on my immediate left, I notice the broom and the dustpan leaning against the brick wall. I grab them and run back up the stairs, weirded out by the grim basement.

Upstairs, I pour myself a cup of coffee before I put myself to the cleaning task. If Emily was here, she'd step in and offer to clean up everything. She's good like that: always tries to be helpful and always full of energy. I gaze at the microwave and see it's almost nine, so I rush through the cleaning, tossing the mug pieces into the trash. I take one more sip of coffee and put the mug in the dishwasher, this time slowly so I don't break another one.

Tuesdays and Thursdays are the days I teach. Today is Friday, and I'm grateful I don't need to step in front of the students and face them today. The last thing they did was ludicrous and something I will need to address with them.

In the bathroom, I look at myself in the mirror. My face is looking rough. It's easy to spot that I'd had too many to drink last night. The bags under my eyes look heavy. I run my fingers over them as if that will make them disappear, but the image of the tired me is still there. No one needs to see me today. I'll walk into the university building discretely and hide in my office all day.

CHAPTER 12

"LET'S GO, SCUMBAG."

I am being held from each arm and dragged behind the school. The fourth class has just started, and I can hear the teachers' voices projecting in the classroom for dominance. Obviously, the three of us won't make the class. I observe both of my intruders, and they seem to be in deep contemplation. I've seen them around the school, always together, looking intimidating, as if looking to stir up trouble. One of them has wide shoulders and an enormous head, and his nickname is Bulldog. The other one is taller, imposing, and looking scarier next to Bulldog. The school kids have named him Whiz. Most students know who Bulldog and Whiz are—the menacing couple you want to avoid.

I am not so lucky today.

I don't know where or how far they are taking me. But I go along. There's no reason to show fear or cowardliness just yet. No one from the school can see us, because we're *facing the side with no windows. The forest next to the school gets deeper with distance. I never go there even though my classmates dare me. There's something about the woods I find scary. I've seen too many movies with people getting lost or killed only to be found decades later. Of course, our town doesn't have such statistics, but you never know who can get inspired by a movie.*

As we move farther away from the school, I focus on the flowers along the school fence and the weather. Spring in Vermont comes as fast as winter does, so daffodils and tulips emerge from the ground. There are still a couple of snow patches lingering, but they will disappear soon enough.

"Where are we going?" I ask. I'm trying to sound casual, to make myself a part of their team.

"Shut up, you numb wit," Bulldog says.

His grip on my right side is getting firmer as we move deeper into the woods. It hurts, but I'm afraid to say anything. I look behind my shoulder and see the school getting smaller. Bulldog yanks my arm and tells me to turn around and keep walking. Fast. Faster. I'm feeling the weight of my backpack on my back. It's a lot of burden for a middle-school kid. I'm barely fourteen, and I feel a lot of responsibility hanging on my shoulders.

We walk in silence until the school disappears behind the nearby hill and the trees. They are all evergreen, and they smell heavenly.

"Here," Whiz says. We come to a screeching halt, and

they look around as if to ensure no one's watching us. All around us are trees only, and it's hard to tell how far we are from the nearest house. Danger lurks in the air, and my mind is running through the worst possible scenarios. If I screamed for help, would that do anything? It probably wouldn't, so I do my best to remain calm and await my fate.

Now that we're facing each other head-on, I can see the facial features of the two men a lot better. Or should I call them boys, because that's what they are? Young and still with a lot of growing up and maturing to do. Bulldog looks like he is a professional wrestler. Whiz is built more like me, tall and lean, but you can tell he has the strength of a rock. I'm pretty certain I will never be able to acquire muscles as big as Bulldog's or get strong like Whiz.

Their mean eyes penetrate me. Fear washes over me, because, in my mind, being dragged by two jocks into the woods can't end well. My mind goes back to the scary films in the woods, but I stop myself—it's not helping.

I still don't know what they want, so naïvely, I ask, "What can I do for you, gentlemen?"

They give each other a look and form crooked smiles. "We ain't gentlemen, scumbag." Whiz says. His teeth clench and so do his fists. He looks at me up and down and says, "Nice outfit, douche. Did your rich mom and dad buy it for you?"

My wide eyes stare back at him, and I say nothing.

"Give us your lunch money," Bulldog says.

"I don't have any on me today," I say. Now I see where this is going. If I say I'll have it tomorrow, maybe they'll leave me alone. I continue, "But I'll have it tomo—"

A sudden jab in my stomach makes my body fold. I fall down to the ground. A sharp pain travels through my abs. Then another jab on my side. Then another one. The pain is horrendous, and it's making me dizzy.

On the wet ground, covered in needles, I am lying, my stomach aching terribly. Tears fall down my cheeks, but I cover my face, so they don't see them. I'm already humiliated enough.

"Asshole. Next time we ask you for money, you better have it. You got that?"

I nod and pray to God it will convince them to leave me alone. They stand above me and watch me roll to my side. One of them spits, and the slime lands on my hair. As they drift away from me, their shadowy figures disappear, and a light shines down. Their chatter and laughter subdue. I turn around and watch the trees gently swaying in the sky. Tears travel down my temples and land in my ears. I look for my backpack and see it standing several feet away. Either Bulldog or Whiz kicked it to the side to show one more display of force.

I cup my eyes with my hands, hoping all this might have been a bad dream. A light breeze caresses my face. The faces of the two goons are all too real as I replay the *images. I open my eyes and the trees are still swaying freely. At that moment, I would give everything to be those trees—because the humility and pain befallen on me are too much to bear.*

CHAPTER 13

MY PLAN TO hide from everyone today sounds too good to be true. Murphy's Law kicks in as soon as I enter the premises. When I come into view, a circle of students are in the midst of a conversation, but then it halts. I lower my head as I walk by them, but I can feel their eyes on me. They resume their chatter in a whisper, and I suspect they're talking about me like I'm some kind of celebrity. As I rush through the hallway, a body from around the corner crashes into me.

"Jesus, watch out." I say as I take my glasses off and pinch my nose. We'd butted heads, and the pain throbs through mine. When I look up, Danny is standing in front of me, looking apologetic.

"Doc, I'm so sorry. I didn't know you were coming."

I shake my head in annoyance. I've had enough of Danny the last few days. First whistling, then this.

"You ought to be careful when you turn the corner, for crying out loud."

"I'm so sorry. Please forgive me."

I wave my hand in dismissal and continue walking. Is it no longer safe to walk in the buildings?

When I get to my office, I hoist myself in the chair and close my eyes to compose myself. Things have been rough lately; the last thing I need is a headache. I open up the second drawer and find a Tylenol, pop it in my mouth, and swallow it dry. But my headache worsens when I find an email from William in my inbox. He wants to see me in his office. Again. What does he want this time? I can only hope he wants to apologize for the ways he has treated me lately. He's been curt and unkind.

Someone knocks on my door.

"Come in."

Sarah's head peeks through the door, and she looks at me with her big wide eyes. "Is this a bad time?"

I grunt. It's too late to tell her to leave. I give her a small wave and tell her to come in.

"Hi, Professor Wegner. How are you?"

I've been wondering if Sarah is up to date on the recent happenings on the campus, particularly regarding my standing as a nonentity. She must be. But if she is, she's smart enough to hide it well and pretend like nothing ever happened. She's still counting on the big break with my help when she graduates.

Examining her silently, I'm uncomfortable about my

own physical appearance. My hair is a hot mess, which reminds me I need to find another barbershop. I'm very aware of the effect that too much alcohol has had on my eyes and face. Sarah, on the other hand, is looking different today. Her hair is combed to the side, and there's a certain glow to it. Her eyes are glimmering from the makeup that makes her look fine and graceful, and the red lipstick makes her lips look fuller.

"I hope I'm not disturbing you."

"You're not," I tell her. "Why are you here?"

"I want to discuss our plan for the upcoming conference."

Ah yes. The conference. I've almost forgotten the annual conference on clinical psychology next week. I am supposed to give a brief presentation on my most recent findings on a clinical trial I've been managing with Sarah's help. It's a groundbreaking discovery of how trauma in childhood affects decision making in dire situations. What we offer will delight the community.

"What about it?"

"I was going to book your plane ticket for Monday, but the only flight out of Burlington is at six a.m. Is that okay with you?" Sarah purses her lips and narrows her eyes at me.

"Yeah, yeah. Sure." I say it without giving much thought at all.

She flutters her eyelashes and smiles. "Okay, Prof. I'm looking forward to our trip. You will be great."

I smile back at her, but it doesn't last long.

"Thank you, Sarah. Send me the itinerary when you finish booking the flight."

"Of course. I would never forget."

Sarah heads for the door, and I stop her. "Sarah!"

She turns on her heels and looks at me. "Yes?"

"Do you know of any barbershops in the area?" It's silly, but I want her to know that I do put effort into my appearance.

She gives me another subtle smile. "Of course. There's a really fancy one two blocks from here. I will send you the info."

"Okay."

"I know you want to look dapper for your presentation next week." She winks, turns around, and leaves my office.

Sarah knows how to play her game. If she gets close enough to me, she will get what she has always dreamt of: a glowing recommendation from me. There are only a few things I'd need to do to pull the strings for her. She is acutely aware of my power.

I lean against the chair and close my eyes for a second. Emily comes to mind. A foreboding sense of nostalgia comes over me. I feel we're drifting apart. Maybe a baby will solve our troubles. Having a child together will bond us and create happiness. In all truth, I don't have any proof she is cheating on me.

Not until I see it with my own eyes.

I screw up my nose in disgust at the thought of it and put the thought back in its box before heading for the door. The hallway to William's office is quiet. Fridays are slow and mysterious around here.

Taking a deep breath, I push open the door of William's office and walk into the room. William looks up from his desk and regards me with a stern expression.

"Sit down, Mitch," he says, gesturing to the chair in front of his desk. It's the same chair I've sat on many times before—when I first met William to the time he told me I was a brilliant academic with so much potential to the day he announced I was being tenured, and most recently when we discussed his displeasure in a faculty meeting—but today feels entirely different. It feels more dire, more urgent.

I take a seat and try to keep my voice steady. "What's going on, William? What did you want to talk to me about now?" I stress the word *now*.

William leans forward, clasping his hands together on the desk. "I've heard some more troubling things, Mitch. Things that are very concerning."

My stomach twists in knots. It's not what I expected. In the faintest of hopes, I still saw an apology coming from him, but not this.

"What things?" I ask, my voice barely above a whisper. My fists clench and I force them to relax, but the anger stays in my body. Why does he keep throwing accusations and blame at me?

William looks at me with a mixture of disappointment and frustration. "The incident with the ad hoc exam yesterday. Several students came to my office yesterday to complain. They are not in the best frame of mind to take any exam after hearing about the death of their colleague, classmate, and friend. Surely you understand that? Your action seems punitive. Whatever you are doing has got to stop, Mitch."

William's eyes darken and his teeth clench. All I can think of is those fuckers ratting me out. I hate every and each one.

"I don't need to justify my actions. If they don't like my class, they can withdraw." My voice is calm despite how I'm feeling. I know my stance might jeopardize my position as a faculty in the long run. I am tenured, but I am yet to become a full professor, which ultimately results from hard work, diplomacy, and luck.

"You're a respected member of this university, but your recent behavior is putting all of that in jeopardy. If things continue the way they have been, I'll have no choice but to place you on a leave of absence."

Williams leans on the chair and looks at me with his hostile eyes.

"Is that all?" I say. I don't want to argue with William.

He remains silent and keeps his stare on me. "I've said all I wanted."

I stand and walk away from William's office without a word.

CHAPTER 14

WHEN I RETURN to the office, the email from Sarah awaits. I click on the link to the barbershop and check out the photographs of the fancy-looking interior. In the corner is the telephone number and I pick up the phone and dial. The woman on the other line answers in a cheerful voice and asks how she can help. I tell her I'm in a desperate need of a haircut and I'd like to stop by as soon as possible. She confirms the open slot at four p.m. and bids me a good day.

I have plenty of time until then.

A message from Emily comes through, telling me Emma has booked a restaurant for four people at seven tonight. She gives me the information about the restaurant, that small Italian place downtown where Emily and I used to go for dinner on cold weekends. The staff are friendly and hospitable, and the food is to die for.

I stare at my phone and hit reply: *I have a tight deadline to meet. Please go without me.*

I should feel bad for canceling last minute, since I'd promised Emily I would join, but there's not a slightest speck of guilt inside me. I'm bending the truth for Emily, but she doesn't need to know that. I've canceled on her many times because of my work obligations, and she's always understood. The last thing I want to do is spend time with Brian and Emma and listen to their love stories or be subjected to numerous questions about my job. Especially with this hangover. I don't want to skirt the issues or appear suspicious to Emily. In the past, I could easily tolerate her friends, but they've become a sheer annoyance.

Emily sends a text back immediately. A sad face and: *We will miss you.*

I arrive at the hair salon at exactly four. The place is nearly empty except for a female customer in a corner having hair extensions done. She and her hair stylist are yapping loudly and laughing. The lady who cuts my hair doesn't talk to me, and I appreciate her silence. I'm accustomed to being entertained in the haircutting chair, and I welcome the reprieve from that.

When I walk outside, it's already dark. Instead of heading back to my office, I turn left at the major intersection and continue driving through the desolate town. It's a rare sight to see people around as if an apocalypse has damned the city. People in this town like to hunker down and keep to themselves.

It takes several minutes to drive to my final destination. I pull over and park in front of the building Emily's studio is located in. On the right side is the studio, and next to it, on the left, is Emily's office. Because it's dark, the reflection on the window allows me to see inside, but nobody inside can see me. Emily would never suspect me of spying on her, so I doubt she'd ever look for me at random. Still, I park discretely, away from the building, just in case, but I can see everything clearly.

I peek at the clock and see it's almost five thirty, the time her latest yoga class ends. I can see the entire display of the classroom like a human zoo. Now that the class is over, the ladies in the studio pack up their yoga mats and disburse. One woman approaches Emily and talks to her. Emily seems to listen intently, like she always does, and nods politely. She tilts her head and places her hand on the woman's right hand. She is taking to her, her eyebrows stitched together.

I wonder what they're talking about. Emily has always been a good listener, and I wouldn't be surprised if the woman was confiding in her.

When they conclude their talk, the woman turns around, and I can see that her entire face is covered in a smile. Emily shouts something and waves to everyone lingering in the classroom, then she turns around and leaves. Seconds later, I see her entering her office and stretching her arms. She approaches her desk and grabs the sweatshirt sitting on her chair next to it. When she puts it on, she sits down at her desk and takes out her phone. I can no longer see her face, only the back of her head with a ponytail hanging down her back.

Emily's thumbs are moving fast on the keyboard of her phone. I take out my phone from my pocket and look at it, wondering if she is messaging me again to express her disappointment that I'm not able to join her tonight. To my dismay, she puts her phone on her desk, and nothing comes through on my phone.

The door of her office opens. Emily lifts her head and waves.

A man enters her office and shuts the door behind him as if he is being chased by something outside. I flinch and sit up, leaning forward, my eyes widening.

This must be Miguel.

He's standing in front of her desk and talking to her. His gaze is intensely focused on Emily. He looks tall and muscular, and his facial expression reveals joy and carelessness. Jealousy builds inside me. Emily's ponytail bounces every time she laughs. I know that laugh: full of life, as if no problems in her world exist. He walks around her desk and stands behind her, putting his hand on her right shoulder. Miguel leans and bends a little forward to look at something on her computer screen. He puts his other hand on her left shoulder and massages her slowly.

Emily doesn't flinch or move at his advances; rather, she looks comfortable, as if his action is the norm.

My hands are shaking, and I can no longer stand watching them next to each other. My mind darkens like a cloud in a storm. I can no longer think straight. It's probably best if I turn the engine on and get out of here before I do something I regret.

As I drive home, defeat washes over me. I'm inching closer to believing my wife is cheating on me. I can't provide hard proof, but their closeness and the secret she was asked not to tell are enough for me to come to my verdict.

How have I allowed myself to trust her?

CHAPTER 15

MY DECISION TO stay at home tonight couldn't come at a better time. I can't stand the thought of spending time with Emily after witnessing her and Miguel being so chummy. I've already planned to find entertainment for the night, to get my mind off the scene I'd witnessed earlier. I will watch a movie or take a walk or find a new hobby on a whim. Anything to stop thinking about Emily.

Emily comes home around six, still wearing her usual work attire. I'm sitting on the living room couch and staring at the TV, my feet resting on the coffee table. The local news is on, reporting petty crimes around the town. The weather presenter forecasts a snow storm this weekend. She comes to me and kisses me on the cheek, an old habit. It used to be a kiss on my lips, but months ago, she switched to a less intimate spot. Initially, it didn't bother me, but now I'm pouting at her action and wondering if Miguel is the only one getting lip kisses.

"How was your day?" Before she gives me an opportunity to answer, she yelps, "You got a haircut today! Looks great. Did you see Henry?"

"Yeah." I'm lying because I'm not interested in explaining the reasons I went to another salon. I keep looking straight at the TV in heavy silence.

She senses something is wrong—of course she does—and asks, "Mitch, everything okay?"

Now is the time to tell her about Miguel, but I'm strangely tongue-tied. I don't even know where to begin. Instead, I pretend nothing had happened earlier, that I didn't spy on her, or that I didn't see her and Miguel together in her office.

"Yes, everything's okay. Just a long day."

"Are you sure you don't want to join us tonight? You can have a glass of wine to chill, and then go home to finish up whatever you're working on?"

Her expression is warm, but not overly loving. I doubt her sincerity and I dismiss her by telling her I'm staying home.

"I guess I'll try to be home at a decent time." She walks to the kitchen where she screams, "What happened here?"

I turn my head toward the kitchen and recall breaking the coffee mug earlier today. Her attention to detail has always been impeccable. I think she'd notice if I was missing an eyelash. But I don't respond. There's not much to say except the mug fell on the floor and broke, which she'd already realized.

I can hear the basement door opening, then closing a minute later. Then I hear a commotion in the kitchen, leading me to believe she is re-cleaning the spot I'd already cleaned. Emily's talking to herself, but I can't decipher what she's saying.

Minutes later, she reappears in the living room. "I have to go and get ready for dinner. I don't have much time left." She approaches me and lands another kiss on my cheek.

I attempt to calm my racing mind, but I fail. The images of Emily and Miguel pester me like an annoying mosquito. I take the TV remote and fly through the channels. Nothing is fascinating enough to capture my interest. My foot is fidgeting, and I shift in my seat, my anxiety rising.

Thirty minutes later, she enters the living room, looking dressed and made up. She looks stunning. I can't help but picture Miguel and her, holding hands, standing side by side, giggling together in joy.

I am absolutely terrified of losing her. I can't imagine what my life would be like without her, even though we're clearly not the same couple everyone used to admire and love. We've been together long enough that separation feels like a foreign concept. Maybe a possibility, but neither one would ever even dare to think about it.

"If you change your mind, text me." Her voice comes from the hallway.

"Okay, I will." I manage a smile I hope she can sense in my voice. "Have fun!"

She slams the front door, and all there is left is me and my dark thoughts. I can't concentrate on watching TV, so I go to my office and turn on my computer. I sit there for goodness knows how long. An unsettling feeling propels me to stand up and head toward the foyer. I grab my jacket and the car keys and head out to investigate.

It's pitch-black outside. Even some main streets don't have light poles lined up. The town officials think it's better that way to save money on electricity. Crime here is almost zero, so there's no need to light it up for safety. There is not one soul on the streets of the town. It's Friday evening when most people choose to go out for dinner or socialize with friends at home.

When I arrive at the Italian restaurant, I park outside and see through the window that every table is occupied. The people sitting at a large table in a corner are laughing, while everyone sitting at other tables look solemn. I look for Emily, Emma, and Brian. Strangely, I don't see them. I can see all the tables in the small space, and I look again, but I don't see them. To satisfy my self-doubt, I get out of my car and get close to the restaurant, looking through the glass. I only see the unfamiliar faces and a couple of waiters walking on the floor and carrying trays and plates.

Where is Emily?

Of course, the first thought that comes to mind is that she has abandoned her friends and met with her lover. I look one more time to see if Emma and Brian might be inside, but I don't see them.

I shake my head in disbelief and suddenly have the urge to have a drink. A block from here is Emily's favorite gastro pub. As I stroll down the street towards it, I have a strange feeling that someone is following me. I turn around, but the street is empty. An icy wind picks up and slashes my face. I quicken my steps to run from the cold and arrive at the pub, relieved to be among people. The bar is almost full except for two empty chairs, one in a corner and the other between two couples. I choose the one in the corner and take off my jacket.

The place is lit just enough to see people's faces. The atmosphere is pleasant, with the eighties rock music playing in the background, and it doesn't surprise me Emily likes this pub so much. The bartender approaches me and asks what I want, and I order a beer. He returns within seconds with a pint of a cold IPA.

Just as I tilt my head to have a sip, our eyes meet. She's sitting in a far corner of the restaurant, and even at that distance, I can see her eyes burning with a mix of anger and surprise.

It's Emily.

Her expression changes from surprise to confusion, as she realizes it's me she is looking at. She excuses herself from her friends and makes her way over to me.

"What are you doing here?" she asks, her tone cautious.

"I could ask you the same thing," I reply, though I know I have more explaining to do.

"The Italian restaurant messed up our reservation, so we came here." She's pale and her eyes are filled with something akin to fear. She continues to probe. "I thought you were working tonight. I don't understand, Mitch."

Emily is rarely rattled, but she is looking enraged. She's shaking and she keeps clenching and unclenching her fists.

"Why don't you go have fun with your friends, and I will see you at home?" My voice is bubbly, attempting to deescalate the situation. As I encourage her to go back to her friends, I gesture at the far table where Emma and Brian are staring at their phones.

"Fine!" she yelps.

Emily turns around and walks slowly yet deliberately back to the table. I watch her move with elegance and grace, even as she boils from rage. She sits down and gives me one last look, then gazes at her friends and smiles. I drink my beer in one gulp, leave a ten-dollar bill, and exit through the door.

CHAPTER 16

WHEN I ARRIVE HOME, I pour myself a glass of whiskey and hoist myself on the couch. I'm feeling lonely and weird and anxious about Emily's arrival home. I replay the scenario in the pub over and over and keep telling myself it shouldn't be a big deal. Emily can't be too upset about the trivial encounter at the pub.

I am so wrong.

As soon as Emily arrives home after her dinner with friends, she storms into the living room without saying hello and barrages me with questions. When she talks, her face reddens with anger, though her eyes remain soft. I don't think Emily can ever become a raging lunatic, even if she tries.

"What were you thinking, Mitch? You embarrassed the hell out of me in front of my friends!"

Her voice echoes through the house; a rare occurrence.

By then, I've had a few whiskeys and feel adequately intoxicated. Admittedly, I have been drinking a lot more lately, or precisely since Bradford died. Drinking alcohol seems to be my refuge, a way for me to forget that my life has changed for the worse. I see double Emily as she's standing on the living room floor and gesturing. Her voice is growing in volume. I wonder if she is tipsy, too.

"Your friends are pretentious." I feel like I need to give her an excuse, so this comes out of my mouth.

"What do you mean 'pretentious?' I've known Emma half of my life. She's a decent human being."

"Yeah, well. If she were so decent, why is she marrying that douche?"

She stares at me as if in disbelief. "What douche? Brian? Brian is the nicest guy ever! They are good for each other. And besides, who are you to judge them, Mitch? What's got into you lately?"

I shrug. A lot has happened the last couple of days, but Emily is no longer the person I can trust with my concerns or thoughts. Besides, when I talk, I can hear myself slurring my words and don't want to come across bonkers. If I choose to say anything, it better be tomorrow when I am composed and sober.

"Nothing has gotten into me. What about you? You've been acting all strange the past several days."

"Who? Me?" she widens her eyes and scoffs. "You've gotta be joking. All I do is work, come home, and in between, I spend all my time with you."

As she explains her day-to-day activities, I grow more suspicious of an affair. Why would she have to emphasize her activities if nothing was going on?

"I think there's something you're not telling me."

"What? What am I not telling you, Mitch?" The volume of her voice is rising, another sign of self-preservation.

"I don't know what you're not telling me." I narrow my eyes at her. "I don't think you're the same person I married."

"What?" Tears well up Emily's eyes. Her voice is high-pitched, shaky. "What are you saying?"

I wave at her. I'm not interested in explaining.

"I'm going to bed! You better think about your words, Mitch."

As Emily turns around, I jump off the couch and lunge at her. I turn her around and notice her eyes, wide and scared. Emily lets out a scream, and I put my index finger on my lips and say "Shhh."

With her arms in mine, I push Emily against the closest wall. Fearful eyes set upon me. I can see the reflection of myself in her pupils: large and deformed and determined. I'm giving off an aura of terror. A dash of evil is coming through.

It's only a reflection, I tell myself.

I divert my gaze from my image and refocus on the eyes. Her fear frightens me. I can destroy her—her stature is much smaller than mine—but all I want to do is put a little fear in her, let her know I am weary; make her remember I am her husband.

"Mitch, you're hurting me," she whispers. I hadn't realized I was gripping her wrists so hard—above her head, against the wall—like I'm about to crucify her. I loosen my grip and come closer to her face. My lips land on hers. At first, she doesn't reciprocate. She just stands there, and I can feel her tense body. I can feel her breath, slow and deep, steadied by her self-control. Her eyes dart around like a ball in a pinball machine. It's as if she's waiting for another blow.

I kiss her again. A smile forms on my face. She has capitulated when she kisses me back. I grab her behind and she wraps her legs around me like a little kid hugging a parent, hoping to be protected from something vile. We stare at each other deeply as I carry her to the main bedroom. She is as light as a feather. Her hands run through my hair, and I get goosebumps all over my body. While under the influence, I'm careful not to fall. My body weakens as I carry her up the stairs to the bedroom.

When we arrive in the bedroom, I drop her slowly to the bed and take off her dress. She is lying there in her bra and panties and I'm in absolute awe of her beauty. Emily looks like an angel with her perfect, smooth skin as silky as her long hair caressing her back. Her face looks solemn, measuring my every movement. I get excited and take off my pants, throwing them to the side. Emily is watching me, her expression unchanged. A tear falls from her right eye, then a left one. No sound follows the tears. I wipe them with my hands, smudging them all over her face.

Our bodies melt. Emily moans and whispers something in my ear. I strain to hear the words, but I'm too distracted by the extreme pleasure of the moment. Our anger has melted away and we've flown into the bliss of a perfectly bewildering marriage. After our fight tonight, I've accepted that our marriage will not be the same again.

But I can never come to terms with the fact that Emily is slowly betraying me.

SATURDAY

CHAPTER 17

THE CRUEL SUNSHINE wakes me up in the morning. It's Saturday, but my hangover is forcing me out of bed early. Emily is sleeping with her back turned to me. As I watch her naked body, I'm in awe of her perfectly curved back, as if someone sketched it for a classical painting. I lift the duvet to see the rest of her. Spotting her tight bum arouses me.

An unusual red mark on the bedsheet diverts my eye. It appears to be blood. I rack my brain about what happened last night, but my memory is suddenly brittle and unreliable. I only remember that Emily and I made love, and I thought she'd enjoyed it very much.

Maybe Emily had her period last night, but she didn't want to tell me to appease me. If that's the case, she made the right choice.

I get up and let Emily sleep in. Today, we're heading to her parents' home in the east part of Vermont, an hour and a half ride from our house. Her father, John, is turning seventy today, so they've invited us and their younger daughter, Emily's sister Julie, and her husband Brett, for a little celebration. Our gatherings with her parents have become less frequent as life became busier, but Emily has kept in contact with them frequently to offset that.

Unlike mine, Emily's childhood was what most people would consider normal and uneventful. Her parents are high-school sweethearts, well put together and always kind in their speech. If I am to guess, they have never offended anyone overtly. Emily obviously inherited their kindness, but it's simple to be that way when they have always had a trouble-free, relaxed life. They lived in a suburban house, big enough for the four of them. Her father used to be an engineer, and her mother was a high school teacher until they both retired.

My generation was characterized by couples having children without regard for the consequences. They thought the intention of having children would be enough to call themselves parents, but in reality, they didn't know what rearing children really implied. Same with my parents. I don't remember many happy moments from my childhood. Ever since my father left us, my mother became estranged, not very interested in me as her child. I think she realized, once she'd had me, that she never should have had a child. It is no surprise I don't have a sibling.

My mother was smart enough to learn from her biggest mistake.

Emily was lucky to grow up in a household with her parents' marriage intact. Her childhood was the exception, not a rule. She didn't need to worry about her father up and leaving one day, never to return. She never had to battle with accepting a mother who was drowning in her self-pity and neglecting her child.

I don't know where my father ended up living after he left us, and I don't know if he's still alive. My mother died a couple of years ago, God bless her miserable soul. The day she died, I almost missed her funeral, because a tire blew up on my way, and it took me a while to change it while contending with the deep snow. It was like a bad omen.

Emily's father always wanted her daughter to marry someone reputable, with a suitable career and a decent income. He was relieved when she announced that I, a university professor and a brilliant scholar, had proposed to her. What also helped is that we've known each for a long time, since high school. We lost connection when Emily's parents moved the family to the east part of Vermont. Emily and I kept in touch for a while and didn't reconnect until after graduating from college. After I proposed to Emily, we came for a visit to her parents' house. Her father had brimmed with smiles. He'd sandwiched my hand between his, looked me in the eye, and welcomed me to the family.

But I couldn't care less about the family. I only wanted his daughter.

Now that she's sleeping, I make coffee and watch the morning news on TV. With sleepy eyes, I turn on the coffee machine and head back to the living room, looking for the TV remote.

"What are you looking for?" Emily's voice startles me. I flinch and turn around to see her standing in the middle of the living room.

Her gaze is piercing and intense, and it cuts right through me. She's wearing a long shirt that covers her panties and nothing else. Her long hair looks disheveled, and, with her pale skin, she resembles a creature coming out of a deep well. Her hands are resting on her lower back, and I wonder for the briefest of moments whether she's holding a knife. Her anger is revived with the new day, and there's no doubt she feels like stabbing me now.

I finally muster, "The TV remote."

She scans the room slowly, as if a devil possessed her.

"There." Her finger points at a corner of the couch where the remote is hidden behind a pillow. That hand is empty, but the other one is still resting on her back. I'm careful to move without facing my back to her. It could take seconds for Emily to strike from behind and stab me with the knife.

When I've grabbed the remote, I look up at Emily. But she's no longer standing there. I sigh with relief and go to the kitchen to pour myself coffee.

Am I imagining things? There's no way I'm completely off the mark. The atmosphere in the house has been more uncomfortable lately. It feels like two strangers live together. Emily, for one, doesn't show her morning signs of affection, hugging me from the back and kissing my arms like she used to.

She enters the kitchen and hovers over the kitchen sink, washing her favorite mug. It's a mug she bought when she graduated from Stanford. She's had it for more than a decade. I watch her dutifully scrubbing it while crunching her toes to fight off the cold of the floor.

I lean against the refrigerator while sipping my coffee. Emily approaches the coffee machine and pours the mug. She's behaving as if I'm not in the room. I dart my eyes around and glance at the block of knives sitting in the middle of the island.

They are all there.

"Are you ready for our trip?" Emily remarks, void of feeling.

I sigh with relief that Emily is starting a normal conversation. I don't enjoy having to deal with too much in the morning.

My voice is cheerful when I tell her, "Yeah, I filled up the gas tank last night. It was almost full, but I didn't want to take chances, so I went to the first gas station as soon as I thought about it..."

I'm talking a lot, but Emily says nothing and leaves the kitchen without saying a word. I hear her steps on the stairway and then a shout. "We are leaving in thirty minutes. Be ready!"

My feet slowly move toward the block of knives. I instinctively reach for one and tighten my grip around the handle while my other fist is clenched. I murmur something unintelligible under my breath and release the grip.

I am growing increasingly fearful of my own mind.

CHAPTER 18

SEVERAL MINUTES GO *by before I get up. I stand up with difficulty as if a semi-truck ran over me. My backpack looks beat up and covered in dirt and pine needles. I pick it up, and when I bend down, the stomach pain is still unbearable. I let out a silent screech and head toward the school. It might have made sense to pick the opposite direction, but I'm uncertain where I'd end up if I walked the other way. One thing I know for sure—I don't wish to face my assailants again today.*

I'm walking with a limp, and I need to stop and rest against a tree often. I take twice as long to return. When I arrive at the school, the classes are still ongoing. Instead of waiting for the next one to begin, I keep walking toward my home. I'm terrified that Bulldog and Whiz might jump out of bushes and beat me up again. Will I have to live with this dread, constantly looking out to make sure they don't ambush me?

I come home and go to my room immediately. The house is empty, so I consider myself lucky. I have no desire to face anyone right now or recount my day at school.

It didn't go well. I don't want to be reminded.

The door of my room has a lock, thankfully, so I use it as soon as I enter. The dresser in my room has a mirror, so I approach it and lift my shirt to see the results of today's beatings. A huge red mark on the side of my torso, which I am sure will soon become a black bruise. It's one thing life has gifted me: I bruise easily. Even a strong touch may cause a bruise, so it wouldn't surprise me if it showed up on my arms as well. My plan is to conceal them. I'm going to wear long-sleeved shirts until the blue marks disappear. Nobody needs to know I've been subjected to bullies' game.

In retrospect, it's shameful to admit that I'm the chosen one. I rack my brain to unearth the reasons they've picked me as their target, but nothing comes to mind. As with bullies, their targets are most likely random—no rhyme nor reason for picking one child over another. I've also learned that, well, maybe, they choose a more vulnerable target, someone who won't fight back too much; someone perceived too weak to believe they deserve what they get.

Am I that person?

Maybe. I don't know. At this age, I think I am still discovering myself: my wants, my needs, my long-term life goals.

I'm one of those people who keeps to themselves. At

school, I've become a close friend with a boy my age, Mike. We have similar interests and get along well. I don't consider myself popular or hip by any means. Keeping to myself works for me.

Until it doesn't.

The following day I go to school, I look over my shoulder to see if the two goons are following me. The school is getting a new association for me. It's no longer the place to learn and grow. It's the place where I grow afraid and weary of people like those two bullies.

My friend Mike is home sick today. He woke up with a high fever, so his parents excused him from classes. I usually spent time with him in the hopes those two guys wouldn't dare cross me when I wasn't alone. It's better to keep in herds, no matter how weak an individual is. But Mike can't be much of my protector. His stature is small; he's all skin and bones, and someone could easily break him in one strike. I wouldn't do that to Mike.

The air is clear. I don't see either one of them and I relax my jaw muscles. Yesterday might have been a one-off. Maybe they had a bad day and didn't mean to do what they did. Perhaps they mistook me for someone else. Besides, I'm not rich. My family has simple jobs, a simple house to live in, and lives paycheck to paycheck. But it's all relative, of course. If they think I'm rich, they could very well be on the verge of poverty.

I enter the bathroom and freeze. My two new enemies are standing beside the stall, smoking. They don't flinch when they see me. Bulldog casts a wide smile and spits in the air.

"Hey, ding-dong. You found us."

I reach for the door to open it when Whiz rushes to my side and grabs me by the scruff of my neck. "Where do you think you're going?"

My body tenses up and a surge of fear washes over me. I have barely healed from yesterday's beating, and I'm not ready for more.

"Nowhere," I say in a whisper.

"Good." He is not letting go of me. "Did you bring the money like we asked you to?"

I'm reaching for my pocket, but my arms are in a locked-in position, so I'm having a hard time.

"Yes," I assure him, hoping he'd give me enough room to maneuver. I take a ten-dollar bill out of my pocket and hand it to him. "Here."

He looks at the bill on my palm and screws up his face in disgust. "That's all you've got, punk?"

"Ye-yes." I say. The stuttering is new to me. The power he has over me is undeniable. I want to run away, but I'm frozen in fear.

Bulldog flicks the cigarette butt into the air and approaches us. The sound of him smacking a piece of gum echoes between the walls. He comes to me and punches me in the face. The pain throbs through my skull. I can taste the blood in my mouth, but I am not sure if it's coming from my nose, my mouth, or something else. They are both in my face, smelling of cigarettes and the cologne they think would make him manlier. I want to puke.

Bulldog wants to take another punch when Whiz stops him mid-air. Why he decides to stop him behooves me, but I appreciate the gesture. Whiz grabs me and pushes me to the side to make his pathway through the door clear. As they exit, they tell me they'd see me again tomorrow and I'd better prepare my lunch money for them.

That's when I knew I was their permanent target.

That's when my life turned for the worse.

CHAPTER 19

THE RIDE to the other side of the state is a little less than two hours. I am driving while Emily is sitting in the passenger seat, looking ahead, pensive. She has sunglasses on, so I can't tell exactly what's behind them. I gaze at her once in a while, when the road is not too windy, and look for signs of distress, relief, or anything that would point me at how she feels about last night. But she is looking stoic, disengaged, quiet.

The scenic roads are my choice for the day; there's something about the Vermont greenery that brings calm to the eye. It will take us longer to get there, but I'm buying myself time to smooth things over between Emily and me. She's been acting strange this morning, and I don't want her parents to sense the tension between us. Her father always senses even the smallest trace of Emily's distress and presses her to tell him what's going on until he solves her problems.

The silence is irking me, so I turn on the radio. The nineties music plays, and I turn down the volume. Emily turns her head toward me and then right back ahead of her again, not saying a word. She seems undisturbed by the disruption of silence.

Her hands are resting on her lap. The engagement ring I carefully picked for her is shining brightly against the sun's rays. It reminds of the days Emily and I reunited, and how we connected almost immediately.

Emily and I both attended the same high school and were from the same town, but our social circles were different. We would say hello to one another as we passed, but we had no common friends and we never hung out together. Eventually, I noticed Emily had disappeared, and that's when I discovered she and her family had shifted to the eastern portion of the state.

Years later, I was waiting in line for ice cream in a small New Hampshire town ice cream shop when I saw Emily standing a few feet away from me. I was fairly certain it was her, but so much time had elapsed since I'd last seen her. I called her name, and when she turned her head in my direction, my jaw dropped. She'd turned into a stunning young woman. When she recognized me, her smile was radiating, and she approached to give me a big hug.

We spent that entire day together. We started off the day on a walk to catch up, then went to a close-by cafe for lunch, and before we knew it, the day had turned into night and we were still together, so we had dinner, too. It felt like no time had passed.

Shortly after, we started dating. At first, Emily and I had a long-distance relationship, but then she joined me in California, which is where I did my clinical work before we tied the knot and returned to Vermont.

As the memories flood me, I have a sudden urge to engage with her.

"Hey," I say.

She looks at me and gives me a smile.

"Hey," she replies.

"Did you enjoy last night?"

She is quiet. It's clear she is pondering her reply. She grabs her ring and twists it around and around.

"Which part?" she says.

She must know I'm referring to the sex part, but there's no doubt she wants to remind me of our fight.

"You really turned me on." I reach for her hand, but she jerks it out of my reach and puts it on the back of her head, her elbow sticking out in my direction.

"I'm glad," she says.

"Everything okay?"

"No."

"What's wrong, honey?"

I am on autopilot with driving, and I'm barely watching the road. Emily has a way of grabbing my full attention.

"In case you need a reminder, I'm still unnerved by your sudden appearance at the pub last night."

I keep silent. I honestly don't know what to say to her. Why does she think it's a big deal? We have some other colossal problems that we must tackle.

"And that's not all," she continues. "You were rough last night. And I didn't like it."

When both Emily and I are sober, our arguments are civil. Her voice is calm and even. Even though she speaks with softness, her choice of words gets to me.

"What do you mean 'rough'?" I want her to explain herself. I'm questioning if the blood mark is linked to this, or if she's alluding to our fight.

My eyes land on her, expecting the answer, when out of nowhere, Emily screams from the top of her lungs, "Mitch, watch out!"

Before I orient myself and see what she means, the collision is already complete. A deer is flying ahead of the car, and I push the brakes as hard as I can to make a hard stop. The airbags fly out of their position and reach both our faces.

By my side, Emily screams, "Oh my god, oh my god."

As she clears the airbag out of her way, I notice fear in her eyes. Surprisingly, her reaction annoys me. I give her a stern look and shake my head. "It's just a deer."

"Just a deer!" she screams. "What do you mean, it's just a deer? We almost got killed, for crying out loud."

"Don't be so dramatic. No one is getting killed over a deer."

We both become silent and look at the animal in front of us. It's lying there, lifeless, with all its extremities spread out. Emily is weeping and her face is covered in tears. She's barely speaking, but she asks, "What should we do?"

"We should call the police. They will know what to do."

"Okay."

I take my phone out and dial 911. On the other side of the line, an operator asks what my emergency is. Getting to my in-laws is definitely not one, so I tell her about the deer.

"Where are you located, sir?"

I look around and don't know what to tell her. "Emily, where are we?" I whisper. She pulls her phone out and google maps us. "Just a second." I tell the operator.

"We're on route fifty-eight, in Lowell," Emily says in a shaky voice.

I repeat the coordinates.

"Okay, sir, we will find you. What's your car damage? Do you need a lift?"

I don't know what the deer did to the car. I storm out of it and walk around. The huge dent in the front startles me. The left wheel is crooked and barely stands on its axis. There's no way I will be able to drive all the way to Newport in this car condition.

"Yes, yes. We will need a lift."

"Do you have triple A or something?

Emily signed us up for it a while ago, thinking ahead of calamities like this one. She has always been thoughtful and proactive about our well-being. We live in Vermont, after all.

"We do. Thank you, I will call them."

The cold outside has shaken my senses, and I realize we might be here for a while. I hope the cops won't take too long to find us. Or that our triple A membership hasn't expired.

As I enter the car, Emily is still crying. She manages to ask me about the car's damage through tears.

"It's nearly totaled," I say. "We need to call triple A to get us home."

"Home? What do you mean, home? We're close to my parents' house, and they'll be so disappointed if we don't come."

"I get that, but we just got into a car accident. They will understand."

"They will, but I won't, Mitch. I want to see my family today. It's my father's birthday, and there's no way I am going to miss it."

I'm quiet for a second, considering our predicament. My fingers involuntarily tap on the door while I stare at the far distance in the front.

"What about the car, Emily? Triple A will need to

drag the car to your parents and then back to our town again. Does that make sense to you?"

"No. We're going to leave the car with my parents. My dad knows a good car body repair shop we can take it to. We can borrow one of their cars and return it when ours is ready."

Emily has always been practical. I turn to look at her. Her face is all flushed and her make-up smudged from crying. I smile. Sometimes I hate how smart she is. I take my wallet out to locate my triple A membership card. I locate the phone on the card and dial.

"Triple A, how may I assist you?"

"Hello. I'm here in the middle of nowhere, stuck with my wife and a dead deer."

Emily no longer looks scared. The anger, disgust, and hatred in her eyes pierce me like a dagger.

CHAPTER 20

THE POLICE SHOW up twenty minutes after the call. They take our license plate and advise us to file the claim with our insurance company. And they take care of the deer. Emily still looks distressed, but a sigh of relief crosses her lips when the triple A tow truck arrives. The triple A driver loads the car onto the lift and tells us to sit in the back of his truck. Emily and I sit next to each other. I'd usually hold her hand in a situation like this, but she appears reserved and pensive.

I leave her alone.

Our driver is a young man and thankfully, not chatty. The atmosphere is heavy, and I don't think either of us would engage in a conversation. He's following the GPS directions to my in-laws' house. Only twenty minutes remain of the ride, but it feels slow, as if the truck is standing and the trees are moving by us, becoming a blur. The silence between my wife and me is excruciating, and

I welcome the truck finally pulling into the house's driveway for the change of scenery.

Emily's mother, Maria, walks through the door with her mouth wide open. She's wearing an open long sweater, holding it at the top with both hands. Last time I saw her was several months ago when her younger daughter, Julie, got married. Her hair looks different; it's no longer combed neatly to one side, and I see some grays sticking out. But there's also something else: she looks a lot older than the last I saw her.

She sees our totaled car on the truck and comes closer to inspect both the car and us.

"What happened, darling?" Her voice sounds panicky. She approaches Emily and embraces her. Emily tightly hugs Maria, as if she's finally getting the comfort she's been yearning for. A hint of jealousy flickers inside me that I'm not the one who can give comfort anymore.

John, Emily's father, joins us. He moves with ease and looks like a vigorous man for his age. The Vermont lifestyle has been good to him. The reason they moved to his part of the state was to get more acreage in their backyard and grow fruits and vegetables. After completing his work for the day, John devotedly takes care of the garden, supplying it with water for his eventual harvest.

Emily runs to his hug, and he kisses her on the side of the head. I stand there, watching the triple A guy fill out a form I need to sign, while Emily explains the collision with the deer.

John looks at me and waves. "Hey, Mitch."

I wave back and say nothing. Emily and her parents enter the house, Emily still rehashing what just happened.

When the Triple A guy finishes the paperwork, he hands it to me and gives me a suspenseful look. "Is she your wife?"

His question has left me speechless since it's not his business. But curiosity takes hold, and I answer to hear what else he has to say.

"Yes, why?"

"That look on her face. Those eyes. I was afraid she was going to strike me from behind." He says. "Good luck, my man."

He hands me the paperwork and jumps into his truck. Without looking in my direction, he drives away with the speed of light.

The moment I go into the house, the warmth is strong, and my glasses are covered in mist. I take them off and wipe them off my shirt. The food smell wafts through the air, promising to be a tasty and delightful meal.

From the corner, Maria comes out to greet me. "Mitch, come on in." She gives me a limp hug and turns around, and I follow her.

Emily's entire nuclear family, plus her sister's husband, Brett, are sitting in the living room surrounding the coffee table. John stands up and gives me a hug, firmer than his wife's.

Emily and Julie are sitting next to each other. Julie

gives me a menacing look as if it's all my fault I hit the deer and jeopardized her sister's life. Do they all blame me for the accident? I give both a quick gaze and notice the facial similarities, except Julie seems to be the uglier version of Emily. It's funny how God rewards one sibling and punishes another. Perhaps it's the look in her eyes that diminishes her beauty.

Brett sits across in a single chair and nods when he sees me. "Hey, Mitch."

I greet him with a wave and say, "Hey, Brett." I turn to Emily's father and wish him a happy birthday. "How does it feel to turn seventy?"

"I'm feeling great, but also acutely aware I have less than half to go." He smiles, but I sense sadness and unsettlement in his voice.

We are all now sitting down, and the conversation has died out since I joined. The atmosphere darkens, as if an impending doom is forthcoming.

Brett turns to me and says, "You okay? Emily was just telling us about the deer collision. That had to be scary."

I look at Emily. She is avoiding my eyes.

"It was definitely unexpected," I say. "But we're still here, luckily."

"Our friend has a car body shop. We can take it to him to get it fixed, don't you worry." Her father reassures us he will help us and take care of it.

I nod and say, "Thank you. That's above and beyond the call of duty."

John lifts his hand and lowers his head. "No trouble. Happy to do it. We're family." He looks at me and smiles. "Besides, retirement has given us a lot of extra time on our hands."

Emily's mother laughs. "Isn't that the truth?" She looks at me with her curious eyes and asks, "How have you been, Mitch? What's new in your world?"

The first thing I think about is Bradford's death and the most current disagreements Emily and I have had, yet I won't tell. I'm here to show the life is as good as I had promised it to be when I first married Emily.

"Good. It's all good. Yeah. Teaching. Going to a conference in a few days."

Emily jerks her head to me and says, "Conference? I don't remember you telling me."

"Darling," I say. "I haven't had a chance to tell you. It's just a two-day trip."

She shakes her head and takes a glass of water in front of her.

"And how's your mother?" my mother-in-law inquires.

I look up quickly and widen my eyes. My palms sweat and my heart picks up a beat.

"My mother has died."

They all look at each other, testing their sanity. Is it possible they've forgotten? They've met her only once, when Emily and I got married, and that was many years ago. Have they misheard what I just said?

"She's dead." I repeat.

"Oh. Mitch." Emily says. "I... we... when did she die?"

Everyone is staring at me, anticipating the answer. I play with my fingers. "I don't know. About a year ago? Maybe two?" I don't mean for my words to appear a question, but they do. They show how unsure and uncaring about my mother's death I am.

"Mitch, why didn't you tell me?" Emily's voice pitches high. She's visibly upset. "Why am I hearing about this just now?"

I have always hated talking about my mother, dead or alive. The day my mother died, I received a phone call from her neighbor, Stephanie, in New Hampshire, where she lived. Stephanie would go visit her often, as is the case in a small community. The day she found my mother dead, she was lying in her bed, arms already crossed on her bosom, as if she knew death was coming. Stephanie noticed a single tear at the corner of my mother's eye that made a trail to her temple. I was teaching when I received the phone call. Emily held the grand opening of her yoga studio that evening. Despite being tired in her bones from all the work she'd done to pull off making her dream come true, her excitement was palpable. She was in her own happy world. I wouldn't have dared to disturb it.

Everyone is staring at me, and the stillness is deepening. They all expect me to say something, but I shrug my shoulders and smile.

Emily's mother gets up from the couch and says,

"Why don't we go to the dining room and eat? The food has been waiting."

They all follow her, except for Emily. She's still sitting on the sofa, her eyes fixated on me. I shake my head and exit the room.

CHAPTER 21

THE DINING TABLE is covered with food. Emily's mother's culinary skills are unparalleled. We're sitting at the table, eating in silence, passing bread and butter to each other back and forth. Emily will sometimes look at me with wide eyes, and other times with a furious glare.

Julie and Brett keep making eye contact, and she appears to be nervous. They're a relatively new couple. Julie is younger than Emily by several years, and about the same as Brett as me. When Julie first introduced us to Brett, they all hoped he and I would hit it off and become best friends, but the opposite happened. Whenever we ran into each other, we'd just give a friendly hello and nothing more. Brett seemed like a good guy, and Julie was his new, most important world, but I had nothing in common with Brett. He grew up in Montana, hunting birds and deer, and now he works as a salesperson in a bike shop. The two of them seem like the epitome of a boring couple. They dress plainly and have nothing interesting to say.

Julie is smiling and looking around the table, then gives a small nod to Brett. They are holding hands resting on the table. Brett gives Julie's hand a light squeeze as a sign of encouragement.

"We have an announcement to make," Julie says.

Everyone stops what they are doing, and stares at Julie. Emily's eyes are wide and bright with expectation.

"Oh," Maria says. "What is it, dear?"

Julie looks at Brett one last time, and he smiles and nods.

"Brett and I are expecting."

A commotion ensues, and everyone is saying something, tripping at each other's voice. I stay silent, watching the couple beaming as they share the news. They all get up on their feet and give each other a hug. I haven't budged out of my chair and don't intend to.

When everyone sits back down and settles in their seat, Maria asks, "When are you due?"

"April," Julie says.

"I can't believe I'm going to be a grandmother. This is the best news I've heard in so long." She tries her best not to crack.

After they answer many more questions, her mother turns to Emily and me, and says, "What about you, Mitch and Emily? Any plans for a baby?"

"Mom." Emily reddens. "Mitch and I will talk about it soon. Please."

I'm surprised and relieved at Emily's statement. Surprised because, given our recent interactions, Emily still wants my baby. Relieved because all the ideas about her infidelity could be just in my head, fogged by everything happening at work. Emily and I have had better times, and I am sure they will return. Every marriage has difficulties, and ours should be no different. Emily and I are yet to arrange a discussion about children.

"You're in your late thirties, darling. You might need to think more seriously about it."

"Mom, please. Late thirties is not too late. Things have changed since you became a mother. Women nowadays bear children in their forties."

"Sure, but you don't want to be that kind of woman, trust me."

I am secretly rooting for her words of encouragement. "You don't want to worry about your teenage kids when you're well in your sixties. It takes lots of energy to raise a child."

"That will be my problem, not yours, Mom."

I notice how Emily says *my* problem, and not *our*. I flinch at that and gaze at her to see the accompanying expression. She looks dignified and stern, and she's not looking at me back. I can't help but wonder if our marriage is more troubled than I realize.

Her father chimes in, "Whatever you decide, we will support you."

Brett cuts off the conversation, as if he has been waiting all along, and says, "Hey, Mitch, please remind me what university you're teaching in?"

"Why?" I shoot back.

"My brother used to go to UV. When I saw him the other day, he said there are rumors a student committed suicide. Do you know anything about that?"

I turn to everyone else, and they are having a deep conversation about something, not paying attention to Brett and me. I sigh in relief, because Bradford's death is still a secret I'm hiding from my wife.

"No," I tell him. "I know nothing about it."

"Hah! Funny. I would think the professors would be aware."

My fists clench under the table and my brows furrow. "Excuse me, I need to use the bathroom."

I dash through the room and into the bathroom, where my furious reflection stares back at me from the mirror. I lower at the sink, open the faucet and splash my face with water. My face is flushed, and I try to relax by moving my jaw around.

When I come out of the bathroom, I see Brett walking by. Instinctively, I plunge toward him and push him against the wall in the narrow hallway.

"What?" Shock forms on Brett's face and it turns into

fear when I push him even harder. I grab him by the collar and come near his face.

"Listen, asshole." Spit flies through my clenched teeth and lands on Brett's face. "Don't breathe to anyone about the student's death, or you're going to regret it."

"I wasn't going to. What the hell is the matter with you?" He is stammering, his eyes bulging at me.

"Good." I let go of Brett, and he straightens his shirt.

"What the fuck, man? You're sick."

I turn around and walk to the dining room, where my wife is laughing with joy.

CHAPTER 22

WE DRIVE HOME THAT EVENING, and the tension between Emily and me hasn't let up. I am being more careful not to hit a deer, so I drive below the speed limit. It's already dark and there is no light projecting from anywhere except for the car's beams. A long, winding road is all we can see in front of us, with woodlands on both sides. It's silent in the car except for the engine revving. Emily's mother lent us her Ford Fiesta until ours gets fixed. Her car makes a peculiar noise, like it needs repair. I'd choose to drive this broken-down car over staying the night at my in-laws.

There's a lot of downtime to think, besides focusing on the road. That Emily doesn't press me about me concealing my mother's death surprises me. I had been expecting a lecture about how I messed up this time. But not one word. Nothing.

I am relieved, but I'm also scared that Emily is caring

less about me and about us as a couple. The prospect of her leaving me fills me with dread, even though our marriage is struggling. I'm scared. I don't want to go back to singlehood and start dating anew.

It's common to turn to familiarity, complacency, even in disadvantageous circumstances.

Halfway into our ride, she speaks up in her stern and self-confident tone, "Let's do dinner tomorrow night and discuss our future family plans."

I turn my head to her and notice she is not looking at me, but at the vista disguised in darkness ahead of us.

"Su-sure." I say.

A sense of hope tingles inside me. Perhaps things will be better once we rehash our plans. I don't see how a baby can't be an object of joy uniting us in love and peace.

"I made a restaurant reservation for tomorrow night." She says it so dryly that I say nothing in response at first.

"Great. I look forward to that," I say. I mean it even though I'm genuinely scared of what our conversation might look like.

"When are you going to the conference?" she says.

"On Monday," I say. "But I'll be back Tuesday evening."

She says nothing, and suspicion creeps in. Does Emily need to know this so she can make plans with her lover? What does she have in store? I bite my lip and hold a tighter grip on the wheel.

I finally muster, "We're good, right?"

I need reassurance Emily will not abandon me.

She remains quiet. I turn my head to her, but I can't see her. It's that dark. Her silence is filling the car, and it's starting to make me feel angry. Emily doesn't answer, perhaps because she doesn't desire an argument while I'm behind the wheel. Could it be that she's trying to control me by ignoring me? I absolutely hate when she does this to me.

I decide to pull a prank on her.

"Watch out! Deer!"

Emily screams from the top of her lungs and leans forward, placing her hands on the glove compartment. Even though I can't actually see her, I can imagine the terror on her face. I burst out laughing, and the sound reverberates in the car.

"What the hell?" Emily screams. "What kind of sick joke are you trying to pull?"

I laugh again. This has her attention, just as I planned. For a second, I weave off the road from laughing, and Emily screams again out of fear we would have another accident. I straighten the wheel and get us back on the right track.

"Relax. It's just a joke," I say calmly.

"What the fuck is your problem? This is not funny! It's not a fucking joke."

I shrug, not that she can see me. Now it's my turn to grow silent. And we stay silent the rest of the way.

As soon as we arrive home, Emily goes to the

bedroom, running up the stairs. I stand at the bottom of the stairs, wondering if I should follow her. The bedroom door slams hard, and that helps me with my decision. I leave Emily alone.

I go to the kitchen to get a glass of whiskey. The day is still relatively young. It's only eight, and I might pick a movie for us to watch. I stop in the middle of the kitchen and grab my phone to text Emily: *What do you want to do tonight?*

I keep looking at my phone, wishing for the three dots, a sign that Emily is typing, but none appear. She's often quick to respond. Sometimes within seconds. I take this as the sign she is going to be angry with me for a while.

But maybe it's me who should be angry at her.

I open the kitchen cabinet to take out a whiskey glass. As I flip it in order to pour myself one, the glass slips out of my hand and drops to the floor, breaking into pieces. This is the second thing I've broken in a matter of days.

I can sense a dark cloud following me everywhere. I feel in my bones something terrible is going to happen.

And soon.

SUNDAY

CHAPTER 23

THE MORNING COMES with a sense of an impending doom.

I try not to think about it too much. After all, today should be a great day. Emily and I are having dinner tonight to discuss our future together and make plans for having a baby soon. It's what keeps me going and hopeful.

I've always wanted a mini-me, someone who I can pass on my smart gene to, someone who will look up to me. It is the reason Emily married me. She didn't want to settle for a shmuck. She and her parents knew she deserved an intellectual, a man well-put together, intelligent and hard-working with a distinguished career. She told me once I was the epitome of success, given all my achievements.

I don't want to mess with her perception of me.

Except for having breakfast in silence, we spend the entire Sunday separately. She goes shopping with Emma, then to lunch, while I stay in my office, preparing for the conference tomorrow. I am putting together a brief slideshow, jotting all of my ideas.

While I'm in the bathroom, washing my face, I hear the front door slam. It's almost five in the afternoon. Emily stands in the living room with a handful of bags on each side. Her face is covered in a wide smile. Shopping seems to energize her and give her life. Her walk-in closet is full of clothes, and I don't think I've ever seen her wear the same garment twice. She knows how to take care of herself, both physically and mentally.

"Hey," I say. "What time is our dinner reservation?"

"At six. I'm going to take a quick shower and we can head out soon." As she walks away, she asks, "How was your day?"

"Good," I say. I want to ask her how hers was, but she has already moved too far away to hear me.

Half an hour later, I go upstairs to change. The water is running in the bathroom. This doesn't seem like a quick shower. Just as that thought crosses my mind, the water faucet shuts, and Emily comes out of the bathroom a minute later. I'm standing in our primary bedroom, not sure what I'm doing.

She shrieks and screams when she sees me, and we are both ridden with fear.

"You scared me! What are you doing here?"

I look around, confused, and shrug my shoulders. "I guess I came upstairs to get ready."

"Be quick. We don't have a lot of time left."

But I'm always quick. I don't need Emily to remind me or tell me this. Her command makes me detest her in this moment, but I shove the feeling aside and walk to my small closet to select clothes for the restaurant.

We both look like a million bucks. I'm wearing my fresh shirt and a pair of khaki pants, and Emily is wearing a black dress with a red scarf over it. Her hair is shiny, and her make-up makes her face look astoundingly beautiful. I come close to her and give her a hug, but she diverts her eyes from me and tells me we better should get going while pushing my hands away.

I squirm at her suggestion, but I dismiss the feeling, fully realizing we have less than ten minutes to get to the restaurant.

Emily has picked a restaurant I have never been to or heard of. It's another surprise she throws at me, and I'm intimated by this discovery. I feel like Emily is leading a whole separate life independent from me, and I'm just there to join the ride whenever is convenient for her.

The restaurant is almost empty, and it's making me anxious. I don't know what it is, I can't put my finger on it, but my palms are sweating, and my heart is racing. Emily looks relaxed, as if she's back at her second or third home.

We sit at a table, facing each other. Now, I realize why I'm anxious. The whole idea of coming to the restaurant to discuss babies is entirely weird. Not the mere space. This was Emily's idea. She wanted us to leave the comfort of our home and discuss a future in a strange place I have never been to. She has caught me off guard, and I don't know what to think of her idea or what it implies. But I oblige. I let her have it despite the voices in my head telling me this is a bad sign.

Emily breaks the silence. Thank goodness, because there is nothing for me to say. She looks comfortable in our new surrounding and I can tell she is completely in command of herself. A hint of relief comes when she recounts her shopping experience today. Halloween is around the corner, and she tells me about the cute costumes she and Emma spotted in a store. I don't care to hear about Halloween, even though I welcome the senseless chatter. My mind is preoccupied with our reason for being here.

We order a bottle of wine, and as soon as it arrives, the waitress fills our glasses. Emily raises hers up in the air and whispers, "Cheers."

I hold my glass and do the same, but I say nothing.

It all feels formal and business-like. Emily is undoubtedly the boss in this situation. Her gaze on me doesn't divert, even when she is drinking wine from the glass. She is too powerful to be reckoned with, and she knows it.

But I don't know how the tables suddenly turned. How did she attain supremacy over me? She has to be a proficient manipulator.

"So," she begins. "I'm glad we're here, finally, to talk about our future." Her face turns mysterious.

"Yes. Me too." I prefer to remain brief. I'll do the listening.

"I'm excited about the prospects of us having a child," Emily continues. I give her a brief smile and return to my solemn expression. "I want us to make sure this is absolutely best for us."

I nod, but I have no clue what she means by it.

"I've decided that I want a child, I do, but having a child will interfere with my business."

My eyes widen in surprise, and I repeat, "Your business?"

She nods a few times and continues, "But I know how much having a child means to you. Trust me, I've thought a lot about this. I'm settled on the idea that we should adopt."

The room spins. This must be a mistake. Emily does want my child. She does want me to be the father of our heir who would look up to me, to us. Anger takes over, and I take my wine glass and take a sip. I hold it so tightly I feel it is going to burst and break in my hand.

"I think you need to explain yourself. This is not the plan we had when we married."

"I know." Her face is sympathetic. "I've thought about what the pregnancy would do to my body. It can't be good for long-term, especially at my age."

"Your age? What age? You're still young, Emily. Women older than you become mothers. I don't see why you would be so different."

"I'm sorry, Mitch. But I will not back out of this idea." Terror covers her face. "I really thought you'd be supportive of this. Don't you think adopting a child would be the same as having our own?"

"Absolutely not." The volume of my voice goes up and a few heads turn around to look at us. "When you adopt a child, you never know what you're going to get. There are a lot of crazy, dumb, uneducated people out there bringing children into the world and turning them into orphans. There are a lot of children abused from birth who will carry trauma their whole life."

As an expert in the field, I know this too well. I've seen so many cases of neglect and abuse that some children never recover from.

"We can work on their issues, Mitch. You make it sound hopeless."

"Well, because it is hopeless. It can be hopeless. These children themselves become abusive monsters, even during their childhood, not to mention when they become adults. You don't want to deal with that. Trust me."

I don't know if Emily will trust me. She seems like she has set her mind firmly on the idea of adopting. But worst of all, I don't know if I can trust Emily anymore. She is certainly not the same person I married. I don't understand how she can be so selfish, thinking only of her needs.

"Mitch, I love you, but lately we haven't had an easy

time in our marriage. Adopt or not, I think we need to work on us first."

I shake my head, but I'm too angry to say anything. The news is unbearable, and it's the only thing that has been on my mind above our marriage.

"What about our child? What about our idea of growing our own family?" I ask desperately.

"You can take it or leave it," she says. A sinister smile forms on her face, and her eyes darken, penetrating mine.

I get up, throwing my napkin against the table. I take one last look at my wife I no longer know or recognize, and storm through the door into the cold, dark night.

CHAPTER 24

THE SCHOOL PRINCIPAL *calls me into his office. I do not know what this is about. Either way, I am dreading facing him.*

I trudge down the corridor, beaten up in sprit and soul. It's been months since those bullies have taken charge of my life. Since then, I've lost some weight, and my grades have worsened.

I sit in the principal's office, my heart racing. I don't know why I am here, but I have a feeling it isn't good. Principal Lewis looks up from his desk and offers me a small smile. He looks like a generous and kind man.

"Thanks for coming in, kiddo." He calls the students "kiddos," and nobody minds. "I wanted to talk to you about your grades," he says in a friendly tone. I am feeling safe around him, but the images of the two monsters tormenting me every day flash in front of my eyes.

I try to relax, but my mind is racing. How did Prin-

cipal Lewis know about my grades? And why does he want to talk to me about them?

"I've noticed that your performance has been slipping," Principal Lewis continues. "Is everything okay at home? Are you feeling okay?"

Well, yes, things at home could be better, but I don't want to talk about it. I nod, not trusting myself to speak. He must not find out what is really going on. I can't risk anyone finding out.

"I'm here to help you. If there's something going on that's making it hard for you to focus on school, I want to know about it," he says, his voice gentle.

I swallow hard, feeling a lump form in my throat. This is it. This is when I have to decide whether to tell the truth or keep the secret locked inside.

"I'm fine," I finally say, my voice barely above a whisper.

Principal Lewis looks at me for a moment, as if he can see through my lie. But then he nods, as if he understands.

"I hear you're good at math. Have you thought about what you want to be when you grow up?"

I live day to day, trying to survive, and don't think about my future. Besides, my zest for math has dissipated lately. I no longer seek to solve math problems outside of class assignments.

I shrug. "I don't know."

"You know, math can take you into many career directions. You can become an engineer, or a math teacher, or *even an astronomer if you choose to do so. If you keep up the studying, you'll be surprised at the rewards you can reap."*

I am looking down at the floor while silence grows between us. The principal clears his throat and says, "Okay. If you need anything, just let me know. We're here to support you." His voice is reassuring.

I get up to leave, feeling a mixture of relief and fear. As I walk out of his office, I know I can't keep the secret forever. But for now, it is all I have to do to protect myself from the bullies who torment me every day.

Bulldog and Whiz have done a number on me. I am ridden with shame. It's one of those things where you feel that maybe, deep down, you deserve to be tormented every day. In retrospect, I know better, because no human being warrants torment, no matter what. Shame has a way of messing you up. I've kept my school experience hushed, like something only the three of us should know. When life gives us something really good or really bad, secrets are the only way to keep it safe. For me, it's all been negative, but I eventually accepted it as the norm. Whenever I go to school, I expect to be slapped around. Whenever I come across the bullies, I expect to give up on whatever they want from me that day.

I'm a prisoner in my own body.

I've pushed my only friend, Mike, away. It's because shame tells me there's a good chance he will reject me as his friend. No, he won't understand. It's not like I've done it consciously. Little by little, my anger has become too much, and he started to avoid me. It's taken him a while to accept the new me and move on from our friendship.

The thing is—I've never accepted the new me. I want to jump out of my skin and start my life anew.

Sadness and lack of self-esteem have replaced fear. It's almost like I have given up on myself. I've kept telling things will get better, and they finally did.

Two of the people I consider my enemies will graduate from middle school and start high school. I am finally free. The last year of the middle school should physically be easier. But the scars are deep, and it doesn't matter they are no longer here. Their shadows will follow me everywhere.

MONDAY

CHAPTER 25

THE FOLLOWING MORNING, I wake up on the couch in my office. After our conversation at dinner last night, I don't want to face Emily. While still dark outside, I sneak into our bedroom to take a pair of underwear and an extra shirt for my trip. I can barely make out Emily's silhouette. Judging by her soft breathing, I can tell she is sleeping peacefully in our bed. She sounds as serene as an innocent child.

I am not accustomed to leave the house without saying goodbye to Emily, no matter what time of morning, but our relationship has come to it. Considering all the fighting we did, I don't think Emily would want a kiss from me.

I leave the house with a heavy heart. It's only five in the morning, and I'm catching the earliest flight to D.C. Sarah is already there; she has gone a day early, so she can spend time with her friend who lives in the city.

The conference provides an opportunity for networking with people with similar interests and exchanging our academic discoveries and thoughts. It's one place that brings out my pride in myself and my accomplishments. All the hard work I have done to achieve this level of success becomes clear when I stand on stage, all eyes peeled on me, watching me, listening to what I have to say.

On the plane, I close my eyes and doze to catch some rest before my presentation. Just as I close my eyes, the airplane hits the ground at seven thirty a.m. The day will be hard and long without the sleep. I have enough time to check in at the hotel and find the conference room, but not enough to take a nap. But, I am pumped about my upcoming presentation and also hungover with dread from the last night. The unsettling feeling is lingering inside me, and I can't shake off the image of Emily and her mysterious eyes when she sat across from me at the table.

I can never forget her threatening gaze, and it seems to follow me wherever I go.

I'm grateful to be away from home. It's a reprieve from all the ugliness that has happened in the last days.

When I go down to the hotel lobby to find the conference room, I run into Sarah. Back on campus, I usually avoid spending time with her, but I find relief in seeing her this morning. She has dressed in a suit and pumps and put on extra makeup to give her a professional appearance. I do a double take as she walks in my direction.

With a huge smile, she approaches me and says, "Hey, Professor Wegner. Nice to see you."

"Yes, nice to see you, too, Sarah."

"I got the conference schedule, and it looks like you are the second presenter on the list."

She hands me a piece of paper, which I assume is the conference agenda. I wave my hand in dismissal. No need for me to be aware of the schedule. I look around, figuring out which direction to take to get to the conference room.

"This way," she says.

Sarah is walking fast, and I'm catching up to her stride. I don't understand why she's rushing, or how she can walk on those heels so fast, but when we arrive, it becomes clearer. The group of presenters is already there and having lively discussions. The breakfast spread and coffee are laid out on a long table up against the wall, and I quickly head to the coffee. Sarah walks up to a group standing in the middle of the room, and chats to them. She has always known how to engage. It's one thing that plays to her advantage.

I stand on the outskirts of the room and watch her gesture while she's speaking. They all laugh in unison. Her charm is irresistible, and I have to be careful not to succumb to it. When I take a sip of my coffee, I feel light-headed. The room spins and I hold on to the wall next to me.

A man walking by me looks at me and says, "Are you okay?"

I don't know what is making him ask me this, but I nod and tell him I'm okay.

"You look pale. You need water or something?"

"No. Really. I am fine." I walk away and find another spot where an intruder is less likely to bother me.

Standing alone in my thoughts, I try to piece together why things at work and my marriage have taken such a steep nosedive, but I can't trace the steps back. Despite my attempts to convince myself that the situation isn't as dire as I believe it to be and that it will eventually be okay, I'm still getting this feeling that it won't.

A commotion in the room ensues, and everyone walks up to the rows of chairs and takes a seat. Sarah is standing in the middle of the room and looking for me. When our eyes meet, she waves me to come near, so we can sit next to each other. My steps feel heavy, but the adrenaline pulsates through my veins.

An older woman with gray, disheveled hair comes on stage and gives us a warm welcome. She speaks through her lisp in a monotone voice, lulling me to boredom. After her speech, she announces the first speaker of the day. A man around my age comes out and gives us a wide smile. I half pay attention to his presentation, my mind focusing on what I am about to say first. When he finishes his presentation, the room clambers in uproar with claps. The gray-haired woman comes out and gives a brief announcement about the next speaker—me.

I stand proudly and give Sarah a brief look. She gives a quick nod and a smile.

When I get on stage, everybody stares at me, and at the moment, my self-awareness becomes so heightened that I freeze. During my presentations, I'm usually animated and confident, darting my eyes around the audience and making connection. I defy the fear of public speaking—the second most common fear next to death. But something has come over me today. I cannot open my mouth. It's as if I've blacked out and no longer have connection to my senses. My hands automatically reach for my temples, and I close my eyes while I massage my head with my index fingers, praying to a higher spirit to rescue me from the situation. Time goes by, and I feel minutes have passed, even though, in reality, it couldn't have been more than seconds.

An aura of agitation lingers in the room until I feel someone move near me. I open my eyes, and it's Sarah standing on the stage next to me.

"Hi, everyone. Dr. Wegner just showed a typical reaction from a person with PTSD in a high-anxiety situation. This is subject to his recent research, and he is here to tell you all about it."

She turns to me, as if expecting me to say something, but my mouth remains shut. My heart races and my palms sweat. All the people in front of me appear to be a blur, and the room spins. I try to take back control, but the downward spiral pulls me in. In the fear or flight response, my legs choose to flee, and I head for the exit as fast as possible. I feel all eyes on me while Sarah distracts the crowd by continuing the presentation. I find the men's bathroom and storm in, shaking from head to toe. With my hands resting on the sink, I'm about to retch. This must be the lowest point of my career.

I am losing control of my life. I need to find a quick way to regain it.

And fast.

CHAPTER 26

AFTER I WASH my face with cold water in the bathroom, the only option I can think of is going to a bar for a drink or two. There is one around the corner from the hotel. I pray it's open at this early hour. When I arrive, my prayers come through. The place looks dumpy, but at least I can be left alone with my thoughts. I sit at the bar and order a shot of whiskey. As soon as the bartender places it on the bar, I pick it up and down it. A tingle of warmth is traveling through my body, and a certain calm comes over me. The bartender tops my glass and I grab it as if someone is about to steal it.

I revisit the event that occurred minutes ago. Is my career over? Maybe it isn't, but I may become the laughingstock among academics. I detest the idea that people who watched my vulnerability on the stage will gossip and recount the tale of a scholar who broke down in front of the entire audience. It is humiliating. If William discovers it, or any of my coworkers, I'm doomed. I'm already under the microscope, thanks to Bradford. They're watching me like I'm an asteroid about to collapse to the Earth. A lot of damage has been done already. I'm hanging by the thread.

Whatever is happening, I'm sure someone is trying to frame me. There's no other explanation.

If I were ever to believe in witchcraft, it would be now. The entire last week has felt as if someone cast a spell on me.

A spell to destroy me.

As I burden myself with these thoughts, someone taps me on my left shoulder. Startled, I turn around to see Sarah standing next to me. Her eyes are sympathetic, and I hate her for it. I don't need her pity. Anyone's pity.

"May I sit?" She gives the chair next to me a gaze and I follow it.

"Sure."

She sits next to me and gives the casual wave to the bartender. A hello wave, not an I-need-something-immediately wave. "How did you find me?"

"It wasn't really difficult."

"What's that supposed to mean?"

"Well, I just assumed you'd want to find a quiet place and get away from everything." She smiles.

Sarah is exceptionally intuitive and smart, which is the reason I hired her as my teaching and research assistant. She chooses the right reaction to every action.

After what happened today, I am curious to know if she will still chase me in pursuit of a recommendation. I wouldn't be surprised if she's changed her mind. Regardless, she is here, and I appreciate her company.

"Your detective work is admirable," I say, but I don't know if she senses my sarcasm.

"I do my best." She laughs.

We sit in silence for most of the time until I feel it is time to leave. I look at my watch and calculate we've been here for two hours. My intake of drinks is usually nearly double what Sarah has had. But spending here two hours has been enough to get drunk, then sober up enough to walk to the hotel. After I settle the bill, I get up from the stool, dizzy from drinking. Sarah jumps to my side and holds onto my arm to help me keep steady. We exit the bar and head to the hotel.

Sarah follows me to my room like a protective little angel. I stumble and wobble at the door, locating the key. When I finally find it and open the door, the need to lie down in bed becomes unsurmountable. I spread out, lying on my back and staring up at the ceiling.

Sarah lies next to me and strokes my leg. "I've missed you," she says. "It's been a while."

She is lying below my waist and looking up at me with her enormous, made-up eyes. Hungry to devour me, she unbuckles my pants and glides them down. She removes my boxers and stares at me, as if she has seen a holy grail. With difficulty, I prop myself and put my elbows on the bed while watching Sarah giving me a sultry look. I grab her hair and pull it towards me. She can't help but let out a shriek when I make my sudden move.

Even though we have done this many times before.

"Who am I?" My words are slurring, but I'm certain Sarah can understand me.

"You are a professor."

"What kind?" I say through my clenched teeth and pull her hair.

"A brilliant one."

"What else?" With each question, I pull her hair harder, and she flinches, fear in her eyes.

"The best kind." I see tears coming out of her eyes, but I keep pressing.

"Am I the sexiest?" Another pull.

"Yes, of course." She's speaking through tears.

"Do I turn you on?" Another pull.

"Yes. Yes, you turn me on."

"You will never think worse of me, no matter what happens?" A big pull.

She screams in response to my pull, and I give her another one, for good measure.

"You're hurting me!"

I let go of her hair and lie back down. "Do it!"

Seconds later, I feel her warm mouth around my penis, but the feeling doesn't travel to my brain or the rest of my body. I can blame it on the alcohol, but I'm not so sure anymore. I fear I'm losing my masculinity, along with everything else I have worked hard for all my life. When I conclude Sarah's strokes do nothing for my pleasure, I tell her to stop. "Get out."

Sarah gets up from the bed and stands facing me. She wipes her nose with her backhand, looking like the ocean just spit her out.

Surely, we must both know this is the end?

She and I have had sex frequently. The first time in my office after we'd finished grading papers. The intellectual stimulation arouses me, so sitting next to Sarah was an easy opportunity to satisfy my needs. Then, every time we went to a conference, a dozen times already, we would go to her or my room and have wild lovemaking sessions. Mostly, we both enjoyed them, although, for whatever reason, Sarah did a lot more work than I did.

But sex with Sarah no longer satisfies me.

I give her one last look before I turn in bed and lie on my stomach. Seconds later, the sound of the door slamming vibrates in my ears.

I should have known that Sarah was about to do the unforgivable.

TUESDAY

I DON'T DARE MOVE out of my room. Until the following day, when I fly back home, I stay put the entire time. I order food for room delivery and watch TV. Sarah doesn't come visit, and I'm not surprised. Emily and I have had sparse communication since my arrival in D.C. until the second day, when I get absolutely nothing from her. In the past, she has taken an interest in my academic activities and often texted me to wish me luck or ask how things went. But this time—crickets. The shifts in my life, my encounters with those around me, have sent me off-kilter.

I am the lone wolf in the forest, suddenly doubting my survival.

Before I leave the hotel room and head to the airport, I take a long shower and bask in tears as I hide behind the water. Since Bradford died, things have changed for the worse, and I'm not the same man anymore.

Maybe I am to blame for his death after all. Maybe I shouldn't have been grading my students so harshly. But it's too late now. The stain on me is too deep and ugly to remove.

My flight to Vermont is relatively short and thankfully uneventful. It's only three in the afternoon when I cross the house threshold. It's quiet in the house, but warm. Emily must still be at work. I cuss under my breath that Emily forgot to turn the heat down before she left for work. Our heating bills go up with the colder weather, and my goal is to always be conscious of our use. Just because our income allows us to splurge, there is no need to waste.

As Emily's return home draws near, my anxiety about seeing her increases. She should be home any minute now, and I put all my energy into being positive.

As I enter the kitchen, my eyes fall upon a surprise. Emily is sitting at the dining table, looking down at her phone. A glass of wine, half full, is sitting on the table. I'm eager to find out why she is absent from work. She lifts her head up from the phone and gazes at me with dark bags around her eyes. She looks as if she hasn't slept all night.

"Hey, honey." Despite my surprise, I greet her in a soft voice.

"Hey," she says.

"What are you doing home so early?"

"Why? When did you start to care about my schedule?"

I see how this is going to go. She will question every word I say, every move I make, from now on.

"Is everything okay? You look tired."

"I wish I could say everything is fine. But nothing seems to be okay anymore, Mitch." Not until I see her better do I realize Emily is intoxicated. She must have been drinking since morning.

"Why? What's wrong?" I ask. She grabs a curled ball of paper sitting next to her and throws it in my direction. It hits my right shoulder and lands in front of my feet. "What is this?"

"I don't know. I'd like to ask you the same."

I bend down and reluctantly grab the paper ball. As I unwrap it, I gaze at Emily, and she looks at me with her menacing eyes. My mind races, trying to figure out what this could be. I can't think of anything. Seconds drift by, yet the weight of the passing time feels like eternity. Emily's stare bores into me, waiting for my reaction as I read.

The note astounds me. I read it and can't believe my eyes.

Your psychopath husband is cheating on you.

My eyes bulge at the note and I jerk my head backwards, hardly able to breathe.

"What is this horseshit?" I say in my defense. My first thought goes to Sarah, who must have told someone about our affair. Even though we finished it on a low note, I don't understand what motivated her to do this. I guess she has nothing to lose. I do. She knows it. She wants to destroy me, take control of our relationship for whatever reasons.

Some kind of ugly revenge.

"Is it true?" Emily's voice cracks.

"No. Of course not."

"Don't lie!" We grow silent for a second. I say nothing. "What about that student who died the other day?"

"What student?" I pretend not to know, but I wonder if Emily can detect another lie seeping through me.

"You think I didn't know about the student, Mitch? Everyone is talking about it! The whole town knows. Where have you been?"

I'm surprised at this, but I shouldn't be. Suicides or murders are not a frequent occurrence in this small town. When they happen, people are rattled, and they panic.

"It's not a big deal," I declare in a casual tone, to subdue the tension.

"What do you mean, it's not a big deal? Aren't you responsible for his death?"

I narrow my eyes at Emily, and anger takes hold of me. I don't appreciate her accusation, and I don't know where all this has come from so suddenly. What has become of Emily? What has happened to my loving wife? I clench my fists and shift my feet.

"You're an asshole! You're ruining our lives!" Emily screams.

She gets up from her chair and lunges toward me. As

she comes nearer, I can smell her alcohol breath. I stop her with both arms up. She makes a step forward and attacks me with her arms, grunting and growling, but I grab her arms and stop her. Emily looks like she's been possessed and doesn't want to let go of me. Her eyes are wide and scary, and her crooked mouth lets out loud growls.

I push her as hard as I can and Emily falls to the floor, her hair covering her face. Stunned, I stand rooted in place, waiting for Emily to execute another move. With difficulty, she gets up from the floor and stares at me with her crazy eyes. As I make a step toward her, she makes a step backward. I'm not paying attention to where or how far she's going, but we are playing the cat-and-mouse game. I suddenly feel like a lion.

Her steps quicken. Before I can tell her to stop, which at the moment I choose not to, Emily takes the first step on the stairway leading to the basement. She seems to have lost control of her balance and takes another fall. She lets out a long screech as she tumbles down the narrow and steep stairs. I can hear her head thump thump thump against the edges of the stairs until all the sound halts, and all is quiet.

I run to the edge of the stairway, and I desperately yell out, "Emily!"

No response.

I switch on the lights and see Emily lying at the bottom of the stairs, her head against the narrow bearing wall. Something dark is surrounding her head, but I can't be sure what it is. Hair or blood. Probably hair. Must be hair.

I call her again, "Emily!"

But Emily doesn't respond. I cap my mouth with my hand in fear the worst has happened to her. I run down the stairway where she is lying peacefully.

"Emily," I whisper. I kneel.

The dark matter isn't her hair.

The blood is still oozing from her head, finding its path out.

I turn Emily around to see her face. Her eyes are wide open, but she's no longer giving the crazy vibe. With my finger, I check out her pulse. Nothing. I bend down and put my face near her mouth, but I don't feel her breathing.

I fly to my feet, heart hammering in my tight chest. What are my next steps? What do I do? Who do I call first?

Is this all my fault?

It's hard to think about anything else now that Emily is dead.

CHAPTER 28

MY HEAD IS DIZZY, and my stomach is churning. I can't concentrate or think clearly. Maybe I should cover Emily with a blanket, but what's the point?

I take a last look at the lifeless Emily before I go upstairs. The blood surrounding her has hardened. It smells like lead. Her body is making strange noises, and for a second, I hope she's alive. But she's not. She can't be. Sounds can still be heard coming from the body after death.

I go upstairs and open up the fringe to see if there is anything to eat. The fridge contains half a dozen eggs, sour cream, a carton of spoiled milk, and leftovers from Emily's Sunday dinner at the restaurant. I'm hungry and I need to eat something before I faint. The leftover Sunday dinner is a piece of chicken and Brussel sprouts. They no longer look appetizing, but I decide to eat them, anyway. Eggs have never been good to my stomach.

After I heat the leftovers in the microwave, I sit at the dining table to eat my meal. Emily's phone is sitting there on the table. At first, I touch it lightly to see if she's gotten any new texts in the past thirty minutes. There's nothing. I take the phone in my hands and try out a couple of different passwords in order to open it. If I unlock her phone, I will see all the little secrets she has kept from me. I'd see all the texts she has exchanged with Miguel. I try a couple of more passwords, but none work. The phone locks me out for five minutes, and I can no longer do anything with this piece of shit. I toss it to the side and eat my meal.

At the least, the chicken and Brussel sprouts are satisfying my hunger. When I finish eating, I put the dirty plate in the sink. It comes to me I must be the one to take on the responsibility of washing dishes since Emily has died. Upon further thought, I realize I am responsible for everything in the house from now on.

Emily is gone.

I go to the bathroom, turn on cold water in the faucet, and splash my face. The coldness invigorates me, and I'm feeling refreshed. In the mirror, my face expression is relaxed. I am ready. I take my phone out of my pocket and dial 911.

"911. What's your emergency?"

"Hi." My voice is calm. "My wife fell down the stairs."

"Is your wife conscious or breathing?"

"No." My voice is steady. "No. I don't think she's breathing."

"Sir, what's your location?"

"I'm at home," I say.

"Where is your home, sir?" I give her our address, twirling my thumb in my shirt. "The police and ambulance should be there shortly."

We hang up and I go sit on the couch. Minutes pass by until I hear the police and ambulance sirens in the distance getting louder. The doorbell rings seconds later and I get up to open the door. A couple of cops and two EMTs are standing on my doorsteps, looking serious.

"Are you Mitch Wegner?" one cop asks me.

"Yes, I am." I wonder if he knows I am a professor.

"May we come in?"

"Of course." I move to the side so they can come in.

"Where is your wife, sir?"

"She's down in the basement."

The two EMTs rush in the direction I show them. The cops are standing in the living room and ask me to sit down. They want to question me.

"Tell us what happened."

"I came home from my trip to D.C. around three. It surprised me to see Emily, my wife, at home. She usually comes home from work later. When I got here, it looked like she'd been drinking all day."

"What was she drinking?"

"Alcohol."

"What type of alcohol?"

"Wine," I say. "Red wine. It was her favorite." I put my head down in disbelief. She is gone. That I'm already talking about my wife in the past tense is slowly sinking in.

"And she was drunk from the red wine?"

I lift my head and look at the cop. "Yes."

"Was she on any medication?"

I slightly lift my head to the left, thinking about whether Emily took any pills. As far as I know, she was healthy and detested poisoning her body with foreign substances. She was all about health. "No."

"Sir, what do you think is the reason for her heavy drinking? Has she had problems or something? Have you two been fighting?" The cop's inquisitive voice is making me uneasy.

I put my head down, thinking of an answer. "No. I mean, yeah. Little fights here and there, but nothing serious. Just petty stuff."

"What kinda petty stuff?" The cop's eyes are burning me. He's studying me, and I feel he is trying to intimate me. But I won't let him.

"You know, small stuff. Who's going to cook dinner, where to go on vacation, putting things away. Typical stupid marriage stuff."

The cop is nodding, but his eyes remain dark and serious. The other cop leaves the living room, and it's just the instigator and me.

"Why do you think she got drunk? Did she have any problems outside your marriage?"

"Problems? I mean, she's had a yoga studio for years, and that might have added to some of her stress. But other than that, I am not aware of any problems." I click my tongue. "Emily and I have been happily married for over ten years."

"When you saw she was drunk, what did you do? Tell me what else happened."

"I was in the living room when it happened. She …" I'm choking and stop to catch a breath. "I heard some noise in the kitchen, but it was very unusual. Not a typical sound you hear every day. When I arrived in the kitchen, I noticed the basement door was open. I knew then."

Tears fill my eyes. As I recount Emily's lifeless body in the basement, I am fully aware I have lost her forever.

He gives a quick nod. "What do you do, sir?"

"I am a college professor." My voice turns proud and confident.

"What do you teach?"

"I teach several psychology classes."

It doesn't occur to me until then they might bring up Bradford's death, of which I am innocent. But what if they think I had something to do with it, like my students do? Will they suspect I am the offender for both deaths?

The two EMTs and the second cop reappear in the living room, the two EMTs carrying a stretcher on which Emily is lying dead. They've covered her whole body with a gray blanket. I cannot see any of her body parts. The EMTs walk out of the house in silence and carry my dead wife into the ambulance. I'm facing the two cops. The one who followed the EMTs gives me a sad look and says, "I'm sorry, sir, your wife has been pronounced dead."

We all know she's dead, but I guess, as a matter of formality, he has to say it.

"I have no further questions," the first cop says. "I'm sorry for your loss, sir. The ambulance will take the body to a morgue, where an autopsy will be done."

They turn around and exit through the door. I stand in the living room, numb.

The dark cloud keeps hanging above me. I wonder what's next.

CHAPTER 29

THE HOUSE SEEMS EERILY quiet without Emily. I'm lost and I don't know what to do with myself. In fact, I'm freaking out. My own thoughts scare me, and I try to shut my mind down to abate them with no success. The images of Emily falling down the stairs and the sounds of her body thumping are things I can't shake off easily. She tumbled down the stairs, making no sounds of her own— no screams, no cries for help, nothing. I wonder what went through her mind before she hit the wall that culminated in her death. Did she think about how to stop? Did she feel anything? Sadness, remorse, relief? Did she know she was about to die? Emily was probably so drunk her body didn't know how to react.

I pace the living room, back and forth, thinking of my next move. I know I should call her parents to let them know, but I am ridden with fear of how to deliver the news. They'll be utterly destroyed.

I hate to be the one to tell them. It's one thing to lose a spouse, but entirely another to lose a child. Spouses we choose consciously mid-life. Sometimes we even get rid of them or replace them, and all is good in life. But children —they are the product of us, something we love and cherish unconditionally. Marriage, at its core, is a conditional agreement. That's why some marriages dissolve: people breach the terms of the agreement, whether they intend to or not.

To ease my nerves, I pour myself a glass of whiskey and down it in a gulp. The heat from the alcohol tingles down my chest. It feels good. The whiskey calms me down, and I'm feeling braver than minutes ago. I'm ready to pick up the phone. So, I do.

The phone rings twice until Emily's mother answers the phone.

"Hello." She sounds cheerful when she hears my voice.

"Hi."

"Hey, Mitch." Her voice has a surprise factor, as if she is curious why I am calling. I never call.

"Hi," I repeat.

"Everything okay? Are you calling about the car?" I'd forgotten all about our damaged car. "It should be ready next Tuesday."

"It's Emily," I say.

Silence. I am feeling the tension even though I haven't spoken the words yet.

"What about Emily?"

Fear and panic seeps from her voice. I am dreading the next moments, but I proceed, because there is no going back.

"Emily has had an accident today. I came home, and she was ... intoxicated." I don't feel the word 'drunk' is respectful at this moment. It is reserved more for students going on a rampage on a spring break. That much Emily deserves.

"Is she okay now?" The panic hasn't left her voice.

"Unfortunately, Emily fell down the basement stairs and hit her head on the wall hard. The fall was so severe that she didn't survive."

Silence. Then I hear a thump and something else, but I can't decipher the sound. Maria remains silent.

She has most likely fainted and dropped her phone, as she fell down. I hang up and decide to call again later.

Minutes later, my telephone rings. It's John, Emily's father.

"Mitch. I see you just talked to Maria on the phone. She's unconscious on the floor. What happened? What did you tell her?"

"It's about Emily. Unfortunately, she fell down the stairs and didn't survive." I clear my throat.

A long beat of silence has me wondering if he has followed suit. "What do you mean? How did that happen?" Her father's voice is cracking.

"She was intoxicated. When I came home from the conference, I found her drinking."

The phone goes dead. I wait for one of them to call me again, but my phone remains silent for the rest of the day.

My mind and body still haven't departed from Emily.

I expect her to come to the living room any moment and give me a kiss and a hug or call me her handsome husband. The physical absence of her still hasn't fully registered with me. I'm yearning for her presence, even though the last week has been the roughest time since we married.

I truly miss her.

I should probably call William and tell him I won't be around at work this week. But I can't bring myself to talk since I have downed a few more glasses of whiskey in less than an hour. My body is feeling tired, and all my thoughts are jumbled together, not making one coherent supposition.

As the whiskey takes over my body and mind, the room spins as I collapse on the couch. To avoid the spiral downfall, I close my eyes to regain control. I feel as if I'm about to throw up.

The black screen appears before my eyes, and I can no longer hold on to reality.

WEDNESDAY

MY HEAD HURTS. I'm in the basement, but I can't remember how I got here or when or why. The basement is dark, except for the faint light coming through the window in the far wall. I'm holding a knife in my hand. The dried blood from Emily is sitting next to me on the floor. I look like I'm in the middle of a murder scene, and I'm the murderer. In a bizarre way, I wonder if I've hurt myself at some point, and maybe that blood is indeed mine, not Emily's. But when I check for wounds on all my body parts, there is absolutely nothing.

What was I doing in the basement? What prompted me to go downstairs? Why am I holding the knife? My mind is vacant, and I remember nothing from last night.

I am moving slowly up the stairs, holding onto the railing. When I arrive in the kitchen, I look through the window and see it's snowing. Halloween is around the corner, but the winter is clearly here. My head is throbbing with pain. Emily keeps a bottle of ibuprofen in the kitchen cabinet for easy access, so I walk to it and take two. I gulp it with a cup of water from the faucet.

Emily's phone is sitting on the dining table. I approach it and push the button to notice several texts from Miguel. He is inquiring about her whereabouts and why she isn't showing up at the studio. *Everything okay?* He seems so caring. I also realize it is eleven in the morning and that shocks me. I must have blacked out last night for a long time.

My phone is ringing. I follow the sound, but it's distant and faint. As I come closer to the living room, I finally see it lying on the floor under the coffee table. It stops ringing. I approach it and kneel to take it. A few missed calls are listed on the phone.

William. Probably wondering why I've not been around the past two days.

Emily's parents. They probably want to arrange a funeral and a wake for Emily. We need to coordinate this effort together.

And another from a number I don't recognize. I push the call back button, and a woman answers the phone. I take a seat on the couch, staring blankly at the TV. I'm tired and disheveled and can feel heavy bags hanging under my eyes.

"Hello?"

"Yes?" the woman on the other side of the line says.

"I received a call from this number earlier today, and I'm calling back."

"Ah, yes. Are you Mr. Wegner?"

"That's me."

"I was calling to inform you that your wife's autopsy results have come in."

Heat rushes to my face, and I struggle to speak.

"Okay ... what are the results?"

"Well, it appears that she was heavily intoxicated at the time of her death. Her blood alcohol level was well above the legal limit."

Silence. I already knew this.

"I'm so sorry for your loss, Mr. Wegner. I also wanted to let you know we discovered something else during the autopsy." My head snaps up and I sit forward, my head spinning. The woman continues, "Your wife was around nine weeks pregnant."

My eyes widen in shock and a wave of emotions crushes me.

"What? That's not possible. She didn't tell me anything about being pregnant."

"I'm sorry, Mr. Wegner. I know this is a difficult time for you, but I wanted to inform you of all the details."

I want to ask her if it's possible to know whose baby it is, but, of course, I am smarter than that. There is no way she would know that. Silence is growing longer, and I don't know what to say.

"Mr. Wegner? Are you still there?"

"Yes."

"If you don't have questions, I'm going to hang up."

I say nothing, and she hangs up, seconds later. My heart is heavy as I sit alone in the living room, surrounded by the remnants of my wife's life. Photos and trinkets on the bookshelf in a corner once held the meaning now feel hollow.

As I try to process the autopsy results that fact that my wife was pregnant, my mind keeps returning to the nagging feeling that something has been off all along. Emily had been acting strange in the week leading up to her death: distant. Definitely distracted. It could have been the hormones that made her behave like a lunatic. There is no doubt now she was hiding something.

But why?

Is it because the baby isn't mine? Was she planning on leaving me?

Maybe the answers lie somewhere in the house. I jump out of the couch and head for Emily's office. Determined to find answers, I sit at Emily's desk and open up her computer. I pause for a second to view her desk. She has a photo of the two of us from the wedding. A photo of us at our honeymoon in Paris. A photo of us camping in New Hampshire. The images prompt my memories to flood, and I remember how blissful our marriage was until recently.

I draw my attention back to her computer. It's not password protected, so I have immediate access to all her files and the browser with all the browsing history. I look at the icons on the desktop and look for any clues leading to her medical records. Maybe she saved the doctor's notes somewhere. But the only icons I see are related to her yoga studio, taxes, and personal stuff. I open up the personal folder, and under it, I see some old letters of mine from when we first started dating over ten years ago. Back then, we sent each other physical notes. I didn't know that she'd scanned them all and saved them on her computer. My letters must have had a sentimental value.

There is nothing about pregnancy. I open up the Safari browser and check out her browsing history. It looks empty. Emily was a neat freak, so I am not surprised to see that she has cleared her browsing history every time she used her computer.

Her desk has a few drawers, so I open up the top one and rummage through it. Finally, there it is. A doctor's note about her upcoming appointment, two weeks from now. I read through the scribbled words and make out the sentences.

Ultrasound results: nine weeks pregnant. Positive heartbeat.

My heart skips a beat. Completely baffled and confused, my mind goes to the worst plausible conclusion: the baby inside Emily wasn't mine. Now I'm fully convinced Emily had an affair with her colleague.

THURSDAY

TODAY IS EMILY'S WAKE, and in two days her funeral. We say last goodbyes.

It's held in a funeral house in Burlington, close to our home. When I arrive, I find my way to the room where Emily's body is resting. The room is full. As well as her family members, she had a lot of friends and acquaintances, and everyone at the yoga studio—employees and students alike—loved her. I scan the room and notice Maria and John standing near the body. John is holding Maria's hand while she's standing there, all dressed in black, with a white handkerchief on her nose, staring at the floor. People approach them to offer condolences, but Maria doesn't even blink. John nods at the people and lets them pass by as they say whatever they are saying.

When they are alone again, I approach them. Maria's eyes are still fixated on the floor, and she looks like a mannequin without movement. John gives me a stern look and says, "Mitch."

I'm at a loss for words, so I scramble to utter these words: "I'm sorry for your loss."

"Stay away from us," he says in a loud whisper.

I widen my eyes at him, and I want to ask him what he means by it, but through the clenched teeth, he repeats, "Stay away. You're dead to us."

He rotates his wife to the right, so they both have their backs turned to me fully. I shake my head, turn around, and walk up to Emily. I watch her tranquil body resting in eternal peace. She's dressed in white and is as pale as her dress. Her eyes are closed, and her arms crossed on her torso. In my distorted mind, I picture Emily waking up and, upon seeing me, giving a smile. A small smile forms on my face as I imagine Emily alive, happy to carry a baby. She'd hug me and tell me a little secret: she is pregnant, and she is having my baby.

I shake off my crazy thoughts. It pains me to know the baby inside her isn't mine.

Somebody taps me on the shoulder, and I turn around to see Emma and Brian standing there. I don't despise them today as much as I usually do. Adversity and tragedy bring people together, acting as a reminder that we will all reach the same end.

"I'm so sorry for your loss, Mitch."

I nod and say, "Thank you, Emma."

Emma looks like she has been crying a great deal. Her

face is saggy, and she doesn't look as pretty as I remember her. She's holding something in her hands, but I can't tell what it is.

"Here. I want you to have this." She extends her arm and hands me a notebook.

"What is it?" I look down and up again at Emma.

"It's Emily's diary from high school. She and I exchanged our diaries before we went to college. We shared everything with each other back then, so there were no surprises." She smiles, as if recollecting the wonderful memories.

I nod a few times and take the notebook from her hand. "Thank you."

Brian is standing next to Emma and says nothing but looks at me with empathetic eyes.

In the room's corner, I notice Julie and Brett standing in silence. Julie is crying while holding her pregnant belly. Her baby will never meet her aunt. Brett, standing next to Julie, is shooting me a menacing look that freezes my blood. I suspect he is holding the grudge from when I attacked him the other day. I wonder what he thinks of me, but there is no time to ponder. I'm here, mourning, without anyone to share the sorrow with. No one, except for Emily's family and a few of her friends, looks familiar. In retrospect, she and I held our lives separately. She had a group of friends, some close and some distant, who she kept in touch with, and I wasn't usually part of that. Some reasons include me, but also, Emily stopped involving me in her social affairs when she realized I had no interest in being a part of it.

Barely anyone else is approaching me to offer their condolences.

Someone taps me on the shoulder again and startles me. I turn around and see a familiar face. I have seen this person before, but I can't remember where.

"Are you Mitch?" the man says. He has a deep voice, and his presence is undeniable.

"I am."

"I'm Miguel." He extends his arm to shake my hand. I look down at his hand and don't offer mine. He grows uncomfortable and pulls his hand when he realizes I have no intention of reciprocating. "I'm sorry for your loss. Emily was a wonderful person."

I nod. He turns to the man standing beside him and says, "This is my partner, Todd."

Todd? A partner? Miguel is gay?

Todd stares at me and says, "I'm sorry for your loss. I've met Emily on a couple of occasions in the yoga studio. She was lovely."

Miguel looks at me with sad eyes and says, "I know you already know all this about her, but she was so loyal. Such a good friend and boss. I could trust her with anything." He gives a small smile, and his eyes fill with tears. "Only recently I'd even told her I was going to propose to Todd and asked her to keep my secret. Which she did, of course." He shakes his head. "She will be so missed."

I feel sick to my stomach. My assumptions about her affair with Miguel have been wrong all along. But even if I try to make things better, it's too late. Emily is gone. A sense of guilt seeps in. I also realize now that the baby inside her has to be mine.

"Excuse me for a second." I run through the crowd and find the men's bathroom in the far corner of the funeral house. I storm into the first stall, shut the door, and lean against it.

Why did she hide the baby from me? And what was she trying to accomplish by taking a copious amount of alcohol the day she died?

Did she want to kill the baby?

That little heart, that beautiful heart that also belonged to me, was already kicking beats. It was alive inside her, growing happy, but Emily kept it from me. None of this makes any sense anymore. I'm hyperventilating and tears are falling down my cheeks.

FRIDAY

TODAY, we bury Emily. After all I've discovered, I'm reluctant to attend the funeral, but I will myself to jump in my car and go. The snow is now deep everywhere, and it will make the funeral more challenging. The cars on the road are driving slowly, and I no longer care if I'm going to get there late.

When I do, the number of people surrounding Emily's grave is cut in half from the previous day. I jump out of my car and approach the burial hole where the casket has been hoisted above. The priest is here, even though I find it laughable since Emily never believed in organized religion or a God. She was a spiritual person who believed a God was in all of us, unique to us and loving. But someone has to send her to the new world and bid her an official farewell regardless of her belief system. It's almost as if the priest's prayers make her departure official and finite.

Her parents and Julie are standing near the casket. They all look gloomy, staring at the casket, still in disbelief that Emily is gone. When I come close, Julie looks at me and diverts her eyes immediately.

The priest begins his prayer and Maria starts to wail. Her voice carries far, and I wonder how long it's going to take her to accept the death of her older daughter. Now I know what it feels like to lose a child. It's not something you'd ever forget.

Or forgive.

I'm lost in my thoughts, and I'm picturing what my baby would look like. In a dream-like manner, I picture myself teaching my child to walk, or say words, or learn about the world. I imagine my child giving me a hug when I come home from work and saying "Daddy!" We play and laugh and the undeniable love for my child is what makes me steady and happy in life.

A smile forms on my face, and I'm feeling stupid because I'm in the middle of burying my wife. I look around to make sure no one saw me. As my eyes dart around, outside the crowd, I see a man standing and looking in my direction. He is wearing a winter hat and sunglasses and a black wool coat. He looks awfully famil-iar, but I can't tell where I have seen him before. It isn't his looks necessarily that give the familiarity away; it's more the way he carries himself. I put my head down and dig through my memory, but nothing is coming to mind.

I shake my head and furrow my brows in frustration

that I can't remember him. When I look up again to see if my memory will win this time, the man in question is walking away. I wait to see what car he will drive in, but he doesn't. He keeps walking until he crosses over a small hill and is no longer in my view.

I draw my attention back to the funeral. A couple of men lower the casket until it makes it to the bottom. Maria's wails are only amplifying. Brett and John are holding her on each side, ensuring she doesn't faint. For a second, I wish I could be that person to comfort, but I know they no longer want anything to do with me.

People throw chunks of dirt onto the casket, and little thumps are heard whenever they land. It's strange to think that Emily's gone forever. I don't join the ritual, but gaze around one more time to see the people's faces. I turn around and walk away, because I have no one to talk to after the funeral, no one to mourn with. When I walk away, no one calls my name or says goodbye.

I am alone.

When I sit at the steering wheel, I take my phone out to see that I've missed several calls from William. I should have told him about my wife, but I suspect he's already found out. This is a small town, and people find out quickly when someone dies.

Especially when their death is early or unexpected.

William didn't leave a voice mail. I tell myself I will call him when I get home. I turn on the engine and proceed toward the main road. The day is looking gloomy, an appropriate reflection of the events taking place inside of it. I turn on the radio and easy classical music is playing. It reminds me of Emily when she used to blast music in the house. Sometimes rock 'n' roll, sometimes classical. She loved life.

Unexpectedly, tears well in my eyes, and they muddle my vision. I wipe them at once and slow down as I drive on the windy roads of Vermont. How am I going to survive alone? The winter is coming, my least favorite season, and I have no one to celebrate the upcoming holidays with. What has my life become?

A phone ring interrupts the classical music. I glance at the screen and see that William is calling me again. He has been trying to reach me for a couple of days now. I never pick up my phone when I drive, so I tell myself I'll call him when I get home.

Home feels empty and cold. I take my phone and see that William finally left a voice mail message.

Mitch, where are you? Call me as soon as you hear this message.

I push the call back button and dial. After only one ring, William answers the phone. He sounds different from what I'm used to.

"Mitch!"

"I was just at my wife's funeral." I say.

"I know. I heard. I'm sorry for your loss." I say nothing, partially because I know he is being diplomatic. "You need to come to the campus as soon as possible."

"I can't."

"Unfortunately, you don't have a choice. You must come."

"Why? What's happening?" An unsettling feeling washes over me.

"It's Sarah." Silence. "Sarah is dead."

CHAPTER 33

SARAH IS DEAD.

William's words are still reverberating in my ears. Apparently, two nights ago, someone stabbed Sarah to death. In the middle of the campus. The coroner's analysis shows she was murdered around midnight, but her body wasn't discovered until around six in the morning. A staff member came in to work early because he had too much work and spotted her body lying helplessly, sitting next to an azalea bush. At first, he thought someone passed out, but when he approached, he noticed blood around the body. He recognized Sarah immediately—she was quite noticeable on campus and was popular among students and staff alike.

It's obvious this was a murder.

But who wanted to kill Sarah? And why? She didn't strike me as confrontational. I don't think she had enemies. The more I ponder about her death, the more

I'm stricken with fear. Sarah died the night I ended up in the basement, holding a knife.

Was it me who killed her while in the blackout? No, it couldn't have been me, because the knife in my hand was clean and blood-free. At least that's what I tell myself. Thinking about it only leads to more confusion and more questions.

This is a second death on campus within days. First Bradford, then Sarah. I can feel it in my bones that something sinister is happening between the university building walls.

After Bradford died, the campus was filled with sadness, but now it has been overtaken by fear and terror. When I enter the building, it's completely empty except for a cop patrolling the hallway as if a war has been declared and they are here to protect us. The students have been told to stay in their dorm room and lock themselves in. They are welcome to call the hotline if they need help to hash things out. Two deaths in several days is a lot to take in.

I hear the patrolling cop's steps move further away and into a distance. When I arrive at my office, there's no reason to unlock it. The door is wide open, and inside, I find William, two university police officers, and the two police officers who'd covered Bradford's suicide. Officer Banks and Officer Moy.

Wide-eyed, I wonder what they're all doing in my

office. The space appears so much smaller with all of them inside. They're standing in a line and staring at me.

William says, "Mitch."

His face expression reveals hopelessness. He knows the most recent two deaths will have a long-lasting effect on the university's reputation. It will be a long road to recovery on many levels.

"Gentlemen," I say. "What are you doing in my office?"

Officer Banks gestures for me to come in. I do, and he approaches the door and closes it.

"Professor Wegner," he says. "It's been a rough week, hasn't it?"

He knows only half of it. I nod. "Yes. It has."

"Is it me, or is it an incredible coincidence that one of your students and your teaching assistant died days from each other?"

"I couldn't agree more."

My stomach ties into a knot. Sarah and I didn't end our affair on a friendly note. But there's more to this puzzle than my brain can conjure right now. Knowing Sarah's good nature, I don't think she was the one who sent the note to Emily. Her writing style is something I know, and this isn't it.

My voice is crackling. "What happened to Sarah?"

"A staff member found Sarah's dead body on a path to the building lot this morning. She'd been lying there for many hours. The autopsy discovered several knife wounds in her abdomen."

Officer Banks stares at me unkindly and studies my every move. I don't react. Though a storm of emotions is going through me.

"Professor Wegner, where were you two nights ago?"

"I was ... I was at home." I say. I don't sound convincing, because that's where I think I was, but now my mind is muddled. That same night, I ended up in the basement of my house, and I couldn't remember anything about it.

Is it possible I have blackouts and do things while in that state and remember nothing in the morning?

Is it possible I killed Sarah? And Bradford?

Can't be.

"What were you doing at home?"

It's a simple question that entirely stumps me. It's slipped my mind. I rack through my brain. "I was resting at home. My wife died several hours earlier."

Officer Banks' brow rises, and he looks at me with disgust. "Your wife just died? Wegner, how did she die?"

I put my head down and avoid eye contact. "She was intoxicated and fell down the stairs."

"You didn't kill her, Wegner, did you?"

I shoot him an angry look and say nothing. He approaches a computer and opens it up. He leans down to find surveillance footage the university has given him access. We're all looking in the computer's direction and watching the footage of a man wearing a mask walking around the building premises. His face, except for the eyes, is covered completely, and there's no way to figure out the true identity. The footage is dark, and the only clear image is a silhouette of a man. His body frame is like mine, the movement familiar.

It terrifies me to know this might be me.

It leaves me speechless. If this is me, I don't remember how I got to the campus and what I did to kill Sarah. How could I be so unaware of my actions? It's true, I've been drinking too much lately. There's a chance that I've been suffering from alcoholic amnesia. It's a state in which a person loses the ability to create fresh memories while still being conscious or awake, yet still able to carry out activities such as walking, talking, and even driving.

Or killing.

I remain silent. William clears his throat and looks like he is about to say something, but he doesn't.

Officer Banks turns to his partner and gives him a quick nod. He pulls a pair of handcuffs from his belt and approaches me.

"Mitch Wegner, you are under arrest. You are the prime suspect of Sarah Winslow's murder."

"What? I didn't do it!" I'm not entirely convinced I am innocent, but it's worth the fight.

He gives me the "you may remain silent" spiel and puts the handcuffs on my wrists. He grabs me by the arm and pulls me toward the door. "Let's go, Wegner."

We exit my office, and I look behind my shoulder.

William is standing by my desk, chewing on his knuckles. His eyes are held in terror. Behind us are Officer Moy and the two university cops who haven't said a word the whole time.

The building is deadly silent, except for our feet moving toward the exit. Officer Banks opens the door, and the winter cold is the only thing I feel. A few students are walking across the campus and when they see me dragged out of the building, they stop to watch us like we're filming a crime movie. They take their phone out and start recording us. I'm sure those videos will circle around the campus in no time. I cringe. My career could be over.

Officer Banks opens the car door in the back and shoves me in. I feel like a caged animal about to be taken to a zoo. Deep down, I believe I'm innocent and all of this is a mistake.

As we drive toward the police station, a blur of houses comes into a vision. I focus on the images and think hard at the same time. The thought becomes as clear as a day.

Someone has been trying to frame me.

CHAPTER 34

OFFICER BANKS PUSHES me into the jail cell. "Get in!" He's rough, but I'm guessing he thinks I don't deserve a better treatment. The cell is a lone room tucked in the corner of the police station. The wall across is covered in white tiles, and the cell is surrounded by cold cement walls. Like every other jail cell, this one is small and is occupied by a single bed, a pisser, and a sink. It smells of mold and staleness, and the stench gives me an instant headache. I don't say anything. Complaining doesn't seem like an option for me.

Officer Banks closes the cell door behind him and watches me through the heavy and thick metal bars. He moves his eyes between the lock and me as if ensuring I remain in the spot. I sit down on the bed and watch Banks making sure the lock is safely in place. He gives me one more look, turns around, and disappears from my view. I hear another door slam, and the space becomes silent.

I seem to be the only person held captive in the police station. Our town is known for low crime, so I wouldn't be surprised if this jail cell has been vacant for a while. I still can't believe it's me who's spending time in here. I have never in my life dreamed I'd be imprisoned someday. Now that I'm lying in the bed with the most uncomfortable mattress, I wonder how long I will be here. Am I guilty of Sarah's murder? Was it me who killed her? How could I have been so careless?

What I do know is that I don't want to spend the rest of my life in jail. I'm yearning for the normalcy of my life where I had a great academic career. I can't get Emily back, but I can go back to teaching and doing research and still contribute to the bettering the world. If I could start all over again, there's little I would change, except the last week. Maybe I would be more sympathetic to my students. Maybe I would have avoided pushing on my agenda with William too much. In retrospect, I was a fool, convinced I was right about everything. And now, here is the price I need to pay. Lack of freedom. Living the life I didn't sign up for.

I shake my head in disbelief.

I'm in search of someone to come to my aid, but I'm still in the dark. My wife is dead, her family disowned me, my ex-lover is dead. The friends I used to have all dissipated when I spent most of my time studying, traveling, or making sure I climbed the career ladder. I doubt they'd have the energy to come and get me out of this place.

I'm imprisoned with my thoughts and nothing else. Where have things gone wrong? My life has taken such a sharp turn for the worse. I wonder if there is redemption on the road.

Time goes by in silence. Without a window in the jail cell, it's hard to tell when it gets dark outside, or what approximate time it could be. Something lulls me to sleep, and I don't know how long I've been sleeping.

The sharp sound of the metal door wakes me up. Officer Banks and another cop I haven't seen before are standing by the cell door.

"Stand up, Wegner," Banks says.

I'm in a slumber, disoriented. What is next? Where are they taking me now? I rub my eyes and stand up as instructed. My eyes are heavy. I approach Officer Banks and instinctively extend my arms so he can handcuff me and take me wherever.

"You're free to go, Wegner." His voice is calm and not so unkind.

I'm surprised and relieved to hear this. "I am?"

"Yes." He looks at me in the eye. "We spoke to your next-door neighbor, and he said he saw you circling around the house at midnight. What the hell were you doing circling around the house?"

"It's an old habit," I say. However, I truly don't know what I was doing circling around the house. This was news to me.

"Your neighbor also said he saw you enter the house

and didn't see or hear you again. It's around the same time Sarah was killed. Consider yourself lucky, Wegner. And thank your neighbor when you see him."

My neighbor is an old man who can be seen peeking through his window twenty-four seven. When Emily and I first moved to this house, his ever-lasting presence and spying on us annoyed us. But then, we eventually learned how to live with it and ignore him when we concluded he was harmless. Who knew that being nosy would pay off someday?

Even though I'm no longer considered the prime suspect, Officer Banks walks me to the exit door with a tight grip under my arm. He releases it when we come close to the door.

"Good luck," he says.

"Thanks."

When he closes the door behind me and walks away, I stand in the police station's parking lot and realize I don't have transportation home. I also can't tell if it's the same day I got arrested or the following day. Everything's a blur.

Despite the minor inconvenience of not having a car, renewed freedom makes me smile. I rub my hands together to generate some heat and put them in the coat's pockets. My car is still parked on the campus and it's some five miles away from the police station. It's going to be a long walk, but worth the effort.

As I take steps forward, the sharp cold cuts through my face. I take a deep breath and exhale.

I am a free man.

CHAPTER 35

THE SNOW SLUSH on the sidewalk is slowing me down. It has snowed the past couple of days. It will probably take me as twice as long to get to the campus, but I continue to walk to my destination. I could call Uber, sure, but I'm determined to walk. This way, I'll have a chance to clear my head maybe, or find solace in being outside in the fresh air.

I take the side roads through the neighborhood and observe the houses on each side. Most of them have been decorated for the upcoming holiday. Children are getting ready to wear their best costume and trick-or-treat.

My thoughts immediately turn to my unborn child. Ever since I found out I would have been a father, I've been consumed with the thoughts of losing my child. I've been daydreaming about what it would be like if the child was born. Every situation involving children I have encountered, I picture my own, growing up to be the source of my joy and happiness. Every time I think of my unborn child, the pain only seems to grow more intense and ferocious. It doesn't seem to subside.

The streets are quiet. The day is at the cusp of being over, and the dusk is settling in with a beautiful purple sunset on the horizon. I am watching the colors blend with the sky, and I am feeling grateful for my freedom. The small things you take for granted are the ones we enjoy the most once we learn captivity. I will never look at the sunset with the same eyes again. I will never breathe the fresh air with the same lungs. I will never walk the street with the same feet.

I tear up, and I tell myself it's from the cold, but I know otherwise. The last couple of weeks have been a whirlwind of activities and emotions. They say, when it rains, it pours. But this is not just a downpour. Some downpours are healthy, like when it's too hot and you need relief from the heat. Or, when your plants are thirsty, and they need water for refreshment and growth. Not this downpour. This downpour is made of deadly spikes and bullets.

Have I done something in the past to deserve it? Has karma caught up to me? I can't recall anything because I'm so engulfed in sadness.

I finally make it to the campus. As I walk through the familiar path I've been on thousands of times before, I can't shake the feeling that someone is watching me. I lift my head and look at the building across, and I think I can see a shadow in one window moving. If my space orientation is correct, that head is peeking from the administrative offices. I stop at the lent Ford Fiesta to see if the shadow will reappear, but it doesn't. I look around one more time and see nothing. I enter the car and head home.

It's already six in the evening, and I'm exhausted from the days before. My stomach is growing from hunger, but I don't have the appetite to eat. I take a hot shower and the effect of the heat tires me more. As soon as I come out of the shower, I crash into our bed. My bed now. I still smell Emily—her sweet scent of perfume that awakens my urge to hug and kiss her. I can't stand the thought of being alone.

I curl up in bed and fall into a deep sleep.

A loud noise wakes me up. I think I heard a glass window shattering downstairs. It feels as if I slept only minutes, but my watch on the nightstand shows a little before midnight.

I'm overly careful when I get up, because I'm suspecting someone is trying to break and enter. On my way down, I look for a weapon in case I need to defend myself against the intruder. But there's nothing.

When I come down, I turn on the lights in the hallway leading to the living room. I think that's where the noise came from, but I can't be sure. The house is empty. I feel a breeze coming in through somewhere, and I notice then the window in the living room is broken. I look down at the floor and see a stone lying there. I am careful not to step on the shattered glass and hurt myself. I go around it and walk up to the window to see if anybody is outside. But I only see my neighbor's house and complete darkness.

My neighbor seems to be awake. I'm surprised he can stay up so late. Do old people no longer sleep? Do they want to enjoy every second left of their life before it's too late?

He's been a widower for decades now, and he never remarried. Apparently, when he and his wife were vacationing, she was lying in a hammock when suddenly a tree branch fell on her and stabbed her in the chest. An instant death. Talk about a freaky way to die. It must have messed up the old man's mind when he lost her so suddenly.

Not that Emily's death wasn't any less freaky.

I slip on my jacket and walk outside. At the door, I see pairs upon pairs of Emily's shoes and boots, and they remind me to get rid of her stuff. Reminders of her only breed more sadness, more pain.

It's dark outside, but with the snow covering the ground, it's easier to discern objects. I walk to the curbside and look for footmarks on the ground leading to my house. The snow is slushy, and any footmarks would have dissipated. I gaze at my neighbor's house and walk up to it. When I find myself on the porch, his front door opens. I don't have a chance to knock.

He's standing at the door and smiling at me. Reduced to a small size and fragile-looking, he has a cane in his hand that he is leaning on. He must have rushed to open up the door, as his mouth is missing dentures.

"Hi," I say.

He nods at me in a jerky way.

"Hello, neighbor." His voice is shaky and high-pitched. The lonely old man must be happy to talk to anyone, as he keeps smiling at me. I have rarely seen any visitors come to his house. When a mailman comes, the old man comes out and chats him up. But I don't think I'm his best choice for socializing.

"Have you seen anyone outside about ten minutes ago? Someone broke my living room window."

He shakes his head slowly and still smiles. His smile is creeping me out, given the seriousness of the situation I am in. Someone just attacked my property, and the old man keeps smiling.

"Did you hear anyone talk or anything like that?" I press even though I suspect I won't get far with him.

"No." He keeps shaking his head.

"Alright," I say with vigor and turn around to leave.

"Wait."

I quickly turn around to face him, hoping he will give me leads or clues.

"I think it was your wife," he whispers.

"Excuse me?"the old man must be crazy.

"Your wife broke the window." His whisper is so low I can barely hear him.

"What the hell?" I say with my teeth clenched. I turn

around and walk to my house. The old man closes the door. I look in the direction of his house and see him peeking out of the window, waving at me.

What a creep.

I go inside the house and duct tape the hole in the window, so at least the cold doesn't come in. When I'm finished, I am too rattled to sleep. I'm debating if I should phone the police and report the break-in, but I'm sure they have had enough of me for now. I go back to bed and jump under the warm covers. My eyes are tired and heavy, but sleep won't be coming any time soon.

CHAPTER 36

PRINCIPAL LEWIS CALLS *me to his office again. What does he want now?*

He looks much less friendly from the last time I visited his office. His forehead is creased, and his lips are tightly pressed together. I stand by his desk and wait for him to instruct me to sit down, but he doesn't. He gets to the point. "I understand you have gotten yourself into trouble yesterday. You struck a young man and got into a fistfight. What is that all about?"

This can't be further from the truth, but I don't argue. The real truth is that Bulldog approached me in the school courtyard yesterday and asked for money. He placed his index finger on my face and started poking me with it. My anger grew so much that I instinctively punched him. My reaction was a shock even to me, because I haven't stood up to my bully until now. He stood there for a few long seconds, in shock I would do something like that, but then his fists took over, and he beat me with them until I fell to the ground.

All my classmates circled us and watched the "fight" unfold. I looked up and saw Mike at the corner of my eye. Terror covered his eyes as he watched me moaning on the ground. No one came up to help me get up. Mike turned around and rushed into the building. His leaving hurt worse than Bulldog's punches. That's when I knew Mike and I would never be good friends again.

"I'm so sorry," I tell Principal Lewis. There's no point in explaining what actually transpired.

"I am very disappointed in you," he hissed. "You were one of the students who held much hope and promise. And look at you now. What has become of you?"

I lower my head in shame. His question must be rhetorical or else it would take a while to explain.

"I must suspend you for a week. Stay home and think about what you've done." He looks at me with anger in eyes. I like him much better when he is soft and understanding. I have had enough of cruelty, though, maybe it's becoming my life.

"Okay."

His eyes widen at me when he realizes I am so agreeable. He slowly shakes his head, as if he is feeling sorry for me. He hands me the suspension note and tells me I am free to go.

The week I stayed home, I had a lot to think about. But one thing kept coming back to mind: what is the perfect plan to turn my fate around?

SATURDAY

CHAPTER 37

DEEP INSIDE, I feel more dread is coming, as if all the doom of the world has leached on to me. I wish I wasn't as paranoid, but it's hard not to be when the world is against me. As I sit at my kitchen dining table and have my morning coffee, I miss Emily. It's strange not to talk for an extended amount of time. We humans need to connect to others, even in the smallest of ways, in order to feel fulfilled and, well ... human. I resolve to move on from everything. I'm ready to turn the page and start my life anew. For the next months, I hope to dedicate my time to something I love dearly: my research and work.

I am behind in my work, but I resolve to return to campus even though I am apprehensive about it. I'm not ready just yet. The possibility of facing my students and other faculty is giving me shivers. My reputation has gone down the drain and I wonder how long it will take for things to normalize. Another generation?

But I can't think of that. I can't torment myself about the fate handed out to the newly deceased. Bradford, my wife, Sarah ... There are still plenty of lives left to save.

The campus is looking glib and deserted. I walk around on eggshells, avoiding people. The police are still working on Sarah's case, trying to demystify who stabbed her and why. They have interviewed several faculty and students, and some staff members, too, but they have gotten no leads. Now Bradford's death seems to be suspicious. They reopened the case, as they suspect that poisoning him might have been a murder after all. There are many tangles the police have not combed out yet. Everyone seems to be anxious, waiting for their turn to be questioned by the police. The campus has never looked as dismal as it does now.

I choose an odd time to go in—on a day classes are not held—so there would be fewer encounters. Luckily, I don't see anyone, and I sneak into my office unseen. It feels like I've been away for years, not days. I look around my office and smile. I've missed it.

My computer is still sitting on my desktop, untouched. I turn it on and try to catch up with the missed emails.

I'm committed to completing the academic paper I began a while back and doing my utmost to stay focused. No one comes to my office to bother me like before. No one cares to check in, no one wants my opinion, no one dares to come in and see how my widowed life is going.

It stings, but I accept it. At least it will be easier to focus.

By the time I finish writing the article, the night has already fallen. I turn around to look through the window and see a few people crossing over the campus. The kids are wearing shorts and sweatshirts in the cold weather, something I'd never been brave enough to do, even at that young age.

I stand up, and my knees buckle. I hold on to the desk to keep steady. Sitting for so many hours at a time can't be good for your health and bones. My stomach, too, signals hunger and I think of a burger and a beer I can order in what used to be Emily's favorite pub. On my way home, I'll stop by and do just that. I tell myself I should start hanging around people more, so I'm not entirely estranged from society.

The main hallway leading to the main exit is quiet. I can hear the whistling in a distance, and I think of Danny, our school janitor. The happy-go-lucky guy loved by everyone in the school. Next time I see him, I'll tell him what a good whistler he is and ask him what his favorite tune is. Maybe that will give me a chance to get to know him better, find out what students like about him so much. Maybe there's one or two things I can learn from him.

Everybody wants to be liked.

Behind me, I hear steps, like a galloping of horses. I turn around to pinpoint where the commotion is coming from, and in a moment I see three men wearing all black, a mask on their face, lunging toward me. My heart is in my throat as they drag me to the nearest bathroom and two guys hold my arms while the third punches and kicks me. I lean against the wall, unable to move. I want to call for help, but every jab knocks a breath out of me. I can't tell who they are or what they want from me, but I suspect I've been on their shit list for a while.

The man punches my face; I taste blood in my mouth. All the strength I had leaves me. I can no longer stand on my feet. The two men holding me release my arms and I fall to the ground like a dead leaf. I feel kicks on my head, my legs, my torso, my arms... It's hard to tell where they all come from. It feels like an army of men is beating me, but as I'm still conscious, and I know it's three men who must hate me. Am I about to die? I won't have enough strength to survive the force. I'm so feeble that not even a glimmer of hope can assist me in defending myself. My eyes dart to the men beating me, but they're completely disguised. Faceless.

The three black figures get blurry in front of my eyes until all I see is complete blackness, and I completely lose my bearing.

CHAPTER 38

WHEN MY EYES OPEN, I wonder if I'm dead. That I've woken up again is a pure miracle. The last time I was conscious, I was pretty certain I was about to die. The last minutes before I went into a blackout, or it could be an injury-induced coma, I was being beaten up badly by three men who had their faces, except for their eyes, covered. That I remember. It's the first thing that comes to mind as I orient myself.

I am lying in bed. The IV is hooked to my body and the heart monitor next to me is beeping. I have recently escaped captivity, and now I've escaped premature death. I consider myself lucky. My body aches. The attackers might have broken several bones, because even a slightest movement brings an incredible pain. I need morphine, something to subdue it. There's no doubt I'm in a hospital —where else would I be hooked on the IV otherwise? Which hospital, what town, how long have I been tied to this bed—I don't have answers to these questions. Soon I'll find out.

I don't know if the medical staff are monitoring my movement, but a few minutes after I wake up, a doctor and a nurse come in. They stand at the bottom of the bed and talk in whispers. They are watching me as if I'm not even awake yet or acknowledging that I am. I muster all the strength I can and wave at them with my fingers. The doctor comes to my bedside and smiles. He looks young and handsome, and suddenly I'm jealous of how vital he looks. This was me until recently.

"How are you doing, Professor Wegner?"

He knows I am a professor. I can't talk even when I try, so I blink twice, hoping he will understand what I'm trying to communicate: I'm happy to live, albeit in an incredible pain.

"Those men got you real good."

I furrow my brow at that comment. They did, and I hope the police find out who they are.

"You have been in a coma for a couple of days. But we've been taking care of you. You also have a couple of broken ribs, and it will take some time for them to heal. The good news is you are pretty healthy otherwise, so you should heal fairly quickly."

I blink twice. That's good news.

"I would say, in a month or two, you'll be like new. But you will need to rest and avoid any strenuous activities."

My lips form a smile. My eyes, too. I can use a month or two to rest. Get away from everything. Reflect. Start my life anew. Whatever that might entail.

"Your friend has been coming to visit every day. He seems like a good friend," the doctor says.

My brows furrow because I am wracking my brain about who that friend could be. As far as I know, I don't have any friends who'd know I'm here, or even visit me while I'm in the hospital. Shoot, I don't have any friends, period. Is it William? When he came to visit, did he call himself a friend?

The doctor looks at his wristwatch and says, "He usually comes around two, so in half an hour. I'm sure he will be happy to see you awake."

So, it's a *he*. I want to ask the doctor what this person has been doing during his visit while I am in a deep coma. I open my mouth, but I remain mute. If he's coming back today, I'll find out soon, I guess.

The anticipation is growing with time, and I'm eager to know who has been calling himself my friend. If my internal clock is as accurate as I think it is, he should visit any time now.

And sure enough—my door opens, and a head peeks through. When he comes through the door, I do a double take, and if I could, I would screech in surprise. What is he doing here?

"Hey, doc."

It's Danny. Our school janitor. The overly friendly

guy. The one I asked to be quiet when he whistled. But I'm perplexed by his visits. We are not friends. Never have been. If I had been in his shoes, I would have had a lot of resentment about being asked to stop whistling. There's got to be a reason he is here. For one, he knows I am here. But how? And why does he care?

There has to be the answer. I hope he will tell me.

I wave with my fingers and blink.

He approaches my bed gingerly and looks around. At the corner of the room is a chair, and he walks up to it and sits down.

We are looking at each other across the room in silence. I don't want him to visit and just stare at me, though. Even in this state, it feels awkward.

A minute or two have passed when Danny opens his mouth and talks. "Glad to see you awake, doc. They told me you were before I came into your room."

Too bad I can't talk. Maybe I could, but I'm tired and in a lot of pain. I don't even attempt. Regardless, I am curious to hear what Danny has to say.

"It was me who found you in the bathroom." He lowers his head and watches his fingers move his cap around. I want to thank him, but I am unable. He looks up with renewed energy and continues, "I called 911 immediately, and they transferred you to the hospital."

I blink twice and smile. That's my way of thanking him.

He shrugs. "You looked pretty lifeless lying on the

floor. I was concerned you wouldn't make it. I picked up an extra shift that day, and I happened to go inside the bathroom when I saw you there."

His eyes darken and settle on mine. "Doc, imagine if I didn't take the shift? Imagine if I wasn't going to take a piss while you were there?"

My eyes furrow. His words have taken on a more urgent tone. Maybe he feels like I owe him something now that he has saved my life. What does he want from me?

"How's your memory, doc?" He raises an eyebrow and stares at me.

There are many kinds of memories: short-term, long-term, sensory, episodic, semantic, procedural, emotional—which one does he mean? I blink once and furrow my brow. I am growing frustrated that I cannot speak. But I want to tell him, memory can be tricky and selective, and we can't always rely on it.

Especially if we experience trauma in life.

"You don't remember me, do you, doc?" He has a smile on his face, but it looks mysterious and forced. I furrow my brow and look down, thinking about where I might have met Danny first. Nothing comes to mind.

Memory indeed can be foggy, especially when we consciously try to forget.

"I'm very disappointed that you don't remember me, doc. My friends call me Danny, but you might know me as Daniel Smith." He pauses and looks at me, as if the closure of his full name will resurface old memories, but it doesn't. I want to apologize if that will give him relief, but I still don't know how I'm at fault for not remembering. "We went to school together, doc. You don't remember. But you know what? I don't blame you. If I were you, I wouldn't remember either. It's been so long."

I don't know what he means by it, but I blink for what seems like forever and hope he will forgive me if forgiveness is needed.

"Well, I'll be on my way out, doc. Maybe you will remember me, maybe you won't." He gives me another inconspicuous smile, gets up from the chair, gives me a small wave, and exits the room.

CHAPTER 39

I AM FOREVER CHANGED.

It all started one day when I was feeling rather low. The school was done for the day, so I walked to the woods in the back and walked around, looking for something to do. The woods turned out to be a bad idea, since nothing but bare trees surrounded me.

I lay down on the ground and watched the trees move in both directions. It was windy that day, but spring came with warmer weather. As I watched the branches, an idea popped into my head. An urge to do something I'd never done before propelled me to get up and head to town.

When I arrived in the town center, a walking distance from school, I entered Seven Eleven in the corner of a block. I reached for my right pocket and found a five-dollar bill I'd brought for lunch this morning. I'd been able to save my money and use it at my leisure lately, because there was no one to steal it from me anymore. At the far wall, I grabbed a bottle of soda from the fridge and a bag of chips from the shelf nearby. The man at the counter looked at me suspiciously, as if I was here to steal. I took my money out, so he could see I was a paying customer, and not some thug.

I grabbed a lighter from the countertop and put it on the pile for the man to ring in. He furrowed his brows. "Do you smoke, young man?"

I shake my head and say, "No, no. It's for my mom. Now that the weather is nicer, she wants to do BBQ outside. She said she was out of matches."

"Ah. That makes sense." The man said with a sense of relief. He was scanning the items as he watched me look at the price come up on the screen. I had enough money to pay.

"You go to school here?" he asked.

"Yes."

"That's good. School is good. Study, so you don't end up like me. Selling random items at a convenience store."

I nodded. I didn't care for the man's advice, but I smiled and thanked him.

After paying, I headed to the hardware store on the other side of the street. I entered and walked around the store until I found what I came here for. At the counter, I placed a can of paint thinner, and the man behind looked at me and said, "Do you have an ID, son?"

"ID? What for?"

"*You need to be eighteen or older to buy this.*" He pointed at the can with his eyes.

"Oh. Well, I'm just buying this for my dad. He wasn't able to drive into town today. He's been sick, so he asked me to buy it for him."

We both stood there and looked at each other. The man was sizing me as if wondering if I was telling the truth. I took my cell phone out and said, "Do you want me to call him? You can talk to him and check."

The man gave a small sigh and shrugged his shoulders. He took the can and scanned it with the price scanner. "That will be nine dollars and fourteen cents."

I sighed with relief. My experience had already taught me about life. It made me wiser and much more acutely aware of how bad or how good people could be. I had a feeling if I tested this man's trustworthiness, he'd voluntarily hand it over.

I took the money out from my left pocket, a twenty, and handed it to him. He still looked at me suspiciously but said nothing. He put the can in a plastic bag and handed it to me with the bill and change in his other hand.

"Thank you," I said.

That evening, I headed to the outskirts of the town where Bulldog lived. I found out where he lived by accident, when I spotted him enter the house without knocking or ringing the bell when I was passing by on the bus one day. I followed him once from school, and it was the same house he went to. It had to be his home. I knew this information about where he lived would come in handy someday.

When I arrived, darkness had enveloped the house and all of its surrounding. In the corner of the backyard, there was a small wooden shed I'd earmarked as my first target. Tiptoeing through the yard, I hid behind the shed and kneeled. I took the paint thinner out of the bag and poured it all over the ground next to the shed. Next, I took the lighter and lit it against the spillage. As soon as the fire from the lighter ignited a small flame, I hopped over the fence and into the next-door neighbor's yard. Then I ran as fast as possible. I looked over my shoulder to see the flame multiplying and traveling quickly. The shed would soon burn down to the ground, and the fire might spread farther.

I ran almost all the way home and entered the house huffing and puffing. I ran to my bedroom, turned the TV on, and waited.

Sometime around seven, the local TV station reported the breaking news. A house on fire. The reporter was standing in the foreground holding a microphone and occasionally turning around to refer to the fire soot. There was no more shed in place of the soot. It had burned down to the foundation.

I turned up the volume to hear what she had to say. "Sometime around six, a fire started in the backyard of this house. The owner's son was at home, but he seemed to not notice the fire until the flame took over the shed. The fire trucks arrived in time to stop the fire spread further, but not soon enough to save the shed." *She pointed her index finger at the place where the shed used to sit.* "The firefighters cannot tell right now the cause of the fire, although they do suspect that a half-lit cigarette butt might have caused it."

Then I remembered—Bulldog smoked. It was a perfect coincidence that played in my favor.

"Ha!" I exclaimed, followed by a loud laughter. I was off the hook. No one would ever suspect it was me who started the fire.

It had been a long time since I'd felt good about myself. Happiness tingled inside me like little butterflies. And it wasn't so much because my arch enemy lost something today. It wasn't about burning the shed to the ground. It wasn't about the fear he might have felt when he first saw the fire. It wasn't even about revenge.

The ultimate thrill was never being found out.

CHAPTER 40

I FEEL blessed that the next day I have the ability to speak. I am regaining strength, and I can already move my arms, albeit not much. The door opens frequently. The doctor and the nurse check on my vitals often as if I am on deathbed. Despite broken ribs and a crushed soul, I am feeling a glimpse of hope. Things can only get better from here.

When the doctor comes in, I ask him what time it is. I am talking, but my words come out in a whisper. I guess I am not ready yet to have a full-on conversation.

He looks at his wristwatch and says, "It's noon. It's almost time for lunch."

I don't care for lunch. The hospital food is some of the worst I have had. It behooves you to realize how much a nightly stay costs, even when the insurance covers part of it, but the food they feed you makes you feel like a stray dog. Sometimes I wonder if a stray dog would eat the shit they serve in a hospital. Thankfully, my appetite is subdued from all the meds I am taking.

The reason I ask the doctor about the time is that I suspect Danny is coming to visit today. Ever since he told me he and I had known each other from before, I've been wracking my brain, attempting to dig in my past.

But no matter how hard I try, my memories are stubborn. I travel through my life in my mind and see if I can spot Danny. My earliest memory is of my mother throwing dishes against the kitchen wall. She and Father had just gotten into a fight. Or, at least, that's what she'd told me. I hadn't witnessed it. She didn't tell me the details; she only said Father was nasty and mean to her. She then got into this unexplainable frenzy where she opened up all the kitchen cabinets and started throwing dish by dish, smashing them into the wall. With each dish, she'd grunt and cuss out Dad.

I didn't know my mother had such a propensity for violence. She'd never struck me that way. But when you are a child, there is not a lot you understand, anyway. I stood in her proximity and watched Mother unravel her rage as I winced at every throw. Once in a while, she'd let out a monstrous scream. I don't know if she realized I was there watching her. It's possible she blanked me out for her own sake.

After that episode, nothing was ever the same again— not my mother, not our lives, and certainly not me. Uncle

Phillip, Mom's brother, took me under his wing and spent as much time as humanly possible with me. He'd take me to parks, festivals, pizza parlors, swimming pools... he took me fishing one time, and I will never forget how carefree we both were. If it weren't for Uncle Phillip, my life would have gone astray, no doubt about that. He was the one to teach me the importance of discipline and getting good grades in school. Uncle Phillip was a former marine, so who else would be better to teach me self-discipline than he?

It's too bad my first memory is of my mother smashing the dishes, not of me and Uncle Phillip sitting at the lake with fish poles in the water, watching the sunset sneak by. What I do know is that living with Mother was the juxtaposition of my time with Uncle Phillip. These two contradicting experiences bred confusion inside me: while living with Mother, I felt like an insecure boy with dreams to live and fulfill, but my mother couldn't care less. But on the other, I had Uncle Phillip walk me through the life and lift my spirits. Who I was and what I meant to others was more of a mystery than a fact. I could be wrong, but based on what I know now about life, I should have been number one. I should have been every single beautiful thing in life. I should have been the most loving son to my mother.

But I wasn't.

Fast-forward to my school days, I dig through my mind to find any traces of Danny. Or Daniel Smith. My school days weren't always roses and flowers. I was a bright kid, but I had little interest in school until Uncle Phillip gave me a serious talk. He was the only influential person in my life whose advice stuck. If it had been my mother offering the same advice, I probably would have told her to buzz off. Uncle Phillip firmly believed education would set me free. And boy, was he right.

I remember a few kids in my middle school: there was Matthew, Matt, who we called Bat. A smart kid, but he was on a chunky side, so he was a loner. The only reason I remember him is that he lived on the other side of our street block, and I'd often see him running with his father up and down, up and down the street. His father was a gym rat and probably ashamed of his plump son.

Then there was Laura. I remember her only because she had the biggest and most beautiful blue eyes I've seen. All the boys had a crush on her, including me, but Laura paid no attention to boys. She was smart and had good grades, and when a teacher asked her to come out and recite a poem in front of us, we'd all silently wow her. Her voice was soothing, and we all loved listening to it.

And then there was the menacing kid we called Bulldog. His nickname was so fitting and appropriate that no one called him by his real name. He was the meanest kid on the planet, and we tried to stay away from him. He enjoyed antagonizing other kids and stealing their lunch money or threatening them if they didn't offer it freely. If

Bulldog didn't consider you your friend, you better steer clear.

I remember some other kids, but they are not as memorable. Daniel Smith never comes up in my memory.

But soon enough, he will be here to visit, and we can have a conversation. I can ask him questions and maybe his answers will help refresh my memory.

When two o'clock comes, I grow nervous and excited all at once. It's hard to believe, but I can't wait to see Danny. He has been punctual, according to my doctor, so he should be opening the door any second. My eyes are wide with anticipation. The minutes are adding up, but Danny isn't walking through the door. He might be stuck in traffic (unlikely at this time of day). Or he might be sick (he looked healthy yesterday). I can think of many other reasons, but speculating gets me only so far.

When an hour passes by, my enthusiasm turns into disappointment. It's clear Danny is a no show today. I close my eyes and continue digging through my memories. The rollercoaster of my life flashes through my mind until it fast-forwards to Emily's funeral. The mysterious man standing outside the crowd is looking more familiar. His coat resembles the one I have seen recently, the one Danny wears. The realization hits me like a punching glove that the mysterious man at my wife's funeral is Danny.

What was he doing there? Was he acquainted with Emily?

Danny made it clear that we'd known each other for a lot longer than a few weeks. I shake my head and tell myself it can't be.

Danny is like an odd puzzle piece that doesn't fit in the jigsaw. But I will find out who he really is.

ONE MONTH LATER

CHAPTER 41

THE DOCTOR DISCHARGES me from the hospital exactly a month after the incident. I'm still feeling brittle and weak, but overall improved from the awful beating. The doctor tells me the ribs have healed, but it will take some time to recoup the full strength.

"Is anyone coming to pick you up?" he says. I feel he is mocking me.

"No." I say. "I'll take an Uber home."

"Take care." He gives me the hospital discharge paperwork, turns around, and walks away.

It's almost Thanksgiving, and I'm feeling nostalgic. Thanksgiving is my favorite holiday. Emily and I used to visit the White Mountains on a Thanksgiving weekend, spending time in front of a fireplace and reading. It was a perfect and relaxing getaway.

The holiday vibes are felt outside. People look relaxed, those together looking lovingly at each other. I think of my home and wonder what I'm going to find. Has it burned down to the foundations? Did someone conspire to destroy my house as they did my life?

When an Uber pulls up at my driveway, I sigh in relief that the house stands as I left it. I look to my neighbor's house, and I think I see him peeking through the window and waving with that creepy smile of his. I wave back out of courtesy and immediately proceed to my house.

When I step inside, it's freezing. I run to turn on the heat and give some life to the place. Everything looks intact, including the broken window covered with duct tape in the living room. I will have to fix it soon before the freezing cold comes and stays for a while.

But maybe I will do more to the house. Maybe I will get rid of all of Emily's stuff: her clothes, her shoes, her pictures, her trinkets, all of her belongings, her toothbrush, all of her hair products, her jewelry, her perfumes, her memories. She had so much. The house is invaded by Emily's things, and I don't want any reminders of her. I can offer all that to Julie, her sister. I have to figure out a way to reach her, since Emily's family has completely disowned me.

Not only will I get rid of Emily's things, but I will also sell all the furniture we used to sit and lie on together. I'll buy new furniture that is just my style—contemporary. I will paint all the walls in different colors. Replace all the kitchen appliances. Finish the basement and bring the ping-pong table and arcade games. Or maybe I won't do any of these things, and simply I do one thing instead: sell the house. I will sell it and get away from this place that reminds me of my dead wife.

There's a house, better than this one, cleaner that this one, more void of memories than this one, that awaits. I want to get away from the creepy old neighbor, too, who watches every move I make. It's time to make a change. Get away from her. From everything.

I go to Emily's walk-in closet and look around. A massive number of dresses and shirts are hanging on the coat rack. Her closet smells like her—that sweet scent of perfume that reminds me of lilacs, that lured me to her embrace, that raises my desire to make love to Emily.

An internal switch is flipped, and my fury is re-energized. I knock all the clothes off the rack. My arms move rapidly, as I get my hands on her clothes. Armfuls of clothes. I run to the backyard and place the clothes on the ground. I make several more trips back and forth until the closet is empty. On my way back to the yard, I stop by the kitchen and grab a bottle of cooking oil and matches. I see Emily's diary Emma gave me at the wake, and I take that with me and add to the pile.

Emily's clothes are sitting in one gigantic pile. Those clothes are worth thousands of dollars, and they could find a home in a goodwill or a thrift shop, if not with Julie, but I can't deal with it. I pour oil all over the pile, light a match, and throw it onto the clothes. A fire catches almost immediately. It rises high in the air and spreads onto the clothes. The heat emanating from the fire is a welcome reprieve against the Vermont cold. I close my eyes and feel the heat hit my face. The remnants of Emily are disappearing in front of me, and I feel the mixed emotions of anger and relief.

Emily is gone, and it is time to accept it for good.

Her clothes are quickly burning and becoming ashes. A black circle of what used to be Emily's belongings is now a symbol of her past. I breathe in and exhale before I head back to the house. In the corner of my eye, the old man is watching me and smiling. I flip him the bird and mouth 'fuck you,' but he doesn't flinch.

I must get away.

CHAPTER 42

I AM surprised how bare the house looks after I get rid of Emily's belongings. I remember when we were first looking to buy a house. We looked at so many properties until we came across this one. It's in a neighborhood of this small Vermont town where houses are considered historic—over two hundred years old. They exude charm and historic mystery. I wanted a contemporary style, but Emily yearned for a quaint charm with lots of history. The houses seemed to be too close, almost on top of each other, but she didn't mind. I asked her if she thought the neighbors might be too close to the house, but she said it was okay. Of the two of us, she was a people lover.

Now that the house is less cluttered, it echoes when I walk through. I feel the surge of hope that, when I go back to work, my life will turn normal. After all, Freud's theory was that the three essential things in life that every human needs to feel happy and fulfilled are love, work, and meaningful relationships. I can at least restore one fast.

I look forward to my days teaching and immersing myself in work. William informed me while I was in the hospital that my classes have been taught by my colleague, a psychology professor, Dr. Matthew Farmer, who is relatively new to the university.

Things have calmed down since the two campus deaths. It remains a mystery what exactly happened. The perpetrator is still out there, and the police are searching desperately, but there have been no developments. The students are worried they might be the next ones, so they've been extra cautious by spending time in their dorm room and staying away from people. The university is not like it used to be—a happy place with a big, joyful family. The campus is covered with a veil of sadness, fear, and mystery. The hotline has never been as busy as now. The students take the liberty to express themselves and their fear of the unknown.

The day I go back to the campus, I drive in my in-laws' car. I will probably never see my old SUV they promised to fix. My car has been sitting in the university parking lot since the day I got beat up. When I get there, the windows look smashed. The vandals not only tried to break me but also everything else I possessed, including my house and my car. I park next to my car and peek inside. There's a lot of trash inside, which isn't mine. Pieces of paper are sitting on the passenger seat. I reach through the broken window, careful not to cut myself, and pick up one piece.

You got what you deserve

I crumple it in my hand and throw it back in the car.

With my head down, I walk toward the campus building where my office is located. The campus looks ghostly and deserted. Many students leave campus to join their family for Thanksgiving. When I arrive in my office, my eyes widen in surprise when I see it wide open. I look around to see if Danny is nearby. Maybe he is doing his cleaning shifts and just got to my office. But I don't see anyone. Perhaps somebody broke in and vandalized it. It's been the norm as of late, so nothing would surprise me anymore. I step inside, and don't see anything unusual. Nothing is missing. Nothing is broken.

I sit in my desk chair and wobble it to feel steadiness, possession, superiority. The desk and the chair and the office, everything inside, still belongs to me. I'm planning on how to move forward in life and make strides at work all over again. Because I'm a professor and an academic.

As I am pondering over this fact, William materializes at the door.

"Mitch," he says.

I wave him in and say, "Come in, William. It's good to see you."

My voice is genuine, and I'm not pretending. I am happy to see William. I've had a strange desire to connect with people again and just to have a simple conversation.

He comes in and closes the door behind him. Worry covers his face, and I can't pinpoint why.

"You shouldn't be here."

"What do you mean, William? This is my office. Where else would I be?"

"That ..." He lowers his head and looks at me again. "I've been trying to contact you with no luck. I've called you and sent you several urgent emails. Now, I know you've been in the hospital the past month, but I was hoping you'd get my messages as soon as you got out."

Now that he mentions phone and email, I realize I've completely failed to check either. I was convinced that no one was there to talk to me.

"Is something wrong? Tell me."

"The university has suspended you indefinitely. A lot of tragedies have happened, and while you are no longer the prime suspect for Bradford's and Sarah's death, it's been quite obvious that your presence is no longer appreciated here."

I'm sitting in my chair with my arms crossed on top of my head and looking at William. Am I hearing things correctly? Suspended indefinitely? How can it be?

"I beg your pardon." I put my head on the chair's armrests and tilt my head. "After all that's happened, you know I am innocent. Right? And the kids who beat me up. What is happening with that? Have the police found them yet? I almost died in that bathroom."

He nods quickly, and I can sense his guilt.

"Listen, Mitch. This is not my decision. I am very sorry. You know I respect your academic achievements and your standard for excellence. But, the truth is, the students hate you and will most likely spread so many rumors about you that nobody will want to take your classes." He pauses for a second and gives me a sad look. "When all this blows over, we can appeal the decision and you can be on campus as soon as next fall."

Next fall. That's an entire year of waiting.

I shake my head. My stomach ties in knots and my heart is racing. Work is my last rescue. But it's been taken from me now.

"Listen to my advice, Mitch. Take a year and do some exploring. Go travel, see the world." He scoffs. "I wish I could do that just about now."

I look up at the ceiling, processing William's words. They sting.

"Okay, William."

"You may no longer be on the campus or in contact with the students. Any violation of this rule will cause revocation of your tenure. Take your time, a couple of hours at the most, and take all your belongings. You're not supposed to be here now at all."

That won't take much. I don't have a lot in my possession in this office.

"There are some boxes outside if you need them. I'm sorry, Mitch. I wish I had better news. But we'll keep in touch, okay?"

He looks at me as if I am a child. I know he is lying. We won't be in touch, and he won't help me repeal the university's decision. He approaches me and stands at my desk. His arm extends toward me, and I take it automatically. "Take care, Mitch."

He releases his hand, turns around, and paces through the door.

I open up my desk and see some notebooks and textbooks I've used for my classes. I open the last draw at the bottom and look for the hidden secret I buried here—Bradford's midterm exam. I move things around to dig it out, but it is not there. Someone must have taken it.

I unplug my computer and take the charger, and place both in my bag. Without hesitation, I walk through the door and don't look back. If I do, I'll break.

As I walk down the hallway, an image in the corner of my eye catches my attention. A man in a chemistry lab is moving about, as if he is looking for something. He's moving slowly and I wonder what he's doing there.

I turn around and mind my own business, walking ahead with a computer under my arm. But an unsettling feeling washes over me when I realize I've seen that man in the chemistry lab before. I turn around and take a few steps back and then I realize: it is him.

The school janitor, Danny.

CHAPTER 43

IT FINALLY HITS me like a heavy brick against my head: Daniel Smith, Danny. I remember exactly who he is! My insides feel like they've been turned upside down.

Fuck!

CHAPTER 44

IT WAS *a matter of time before the police summons arrived.*

My wife wakes up at the sound of my phone and turns around when I tell her to keep sleeping. It's nothing important.

"We need you to come to the police station today." A man on the other line says.

"What is this regarding?" I'm playing dumb.

"It's regarding the two deaths on the Vermont University campus. We need to talk to you."

Why has it taken the police so long to contact me? It's been more than a month since Bradford's and Sarah's deaths. The police must have had no leads and still gathered evidence of the potential murders. The town police are inexperienced in murder cases. This town is not known for a high crime rate. They are much better suited for reporting car collisions with deer or rescuing dogs from a lake.

I have my strong cup of coffee and I get ready by putting on my best suit. A splash of cologne burns my face after I shave.

I arrive at the police station, feeling a strange sense of vigor. My nerves are calm, and I am feeling confident as I approach the front desk.

"I'm here for an interview." I say to the young man behind the desk.

"Your name, sir."

"Daniel Smith."

He checks something on his computer and stands up. "Follow me, sir."

He takes me to a small room in a corner of the police station. I look around, as I've always been curious to see what an interrogation room looks like. I've avoided it so many times, and it makes me smile. The interrogation room is small, and it doesn't have windows. The walls are white and in two corners, there are two video cameras staring in my direction. I look down from the cameras and fix my tie.

A table sits in the middle of the room. There's a chair on one side of the table, and two on the other. The young man instructs me to sit down on the side of the single chair, so I do. I tell myself this is a standard procedure and there's nothing to fear. I have the right to speak to an attorney beforehand, but that's going to be unnecessary.

Minutes later, two detectives walk in. I've seen them

on the campus before. They probably don't recognize me, because I look different wearing a janitor uniform versus a fancy suit an upstanding citizen may wear. They both have a pistol hanging from their belt, but neither one looks stern or scary.

One of them has an audio recorder in his hand that he places on the table.

"Mr. Smith. This is Officer Banks, and I am Officer Moy. We appreciate you coming in today to answer a few questions."

"Of course, anything to help."

"We are going to record this interview." Officer Moy pushes the record button on the recorder and gives me a stern look. "Please state your name."

"Daniel Smith." I am controlling my breathing as I speak.

"What do you do, Mr. Smith?"

"I work as a janitor at the university."

"How long have you worked there?" Officer Moy's eyes are piercing over me.

"I've started working there a few months ago."

"Did you know, or have you ever met, the two victims of the recent murders?"

I pause to think and recall my first interactions with Bradford. One day, I was minding my business and cleaning the cafeteria floor when, out of nowhere, Bradford slams into me and knocks me hard. He didn't use the full *force, but our sudden collision surprised me. I fell down to the floor, and he turned around to look at me. No apology, no nothing.*

"I've seen him around, but we never talked or exchanged words."

"Do you usually do that with students, Mr. Smith?"

"Yes, but the students usually start a conversation with me. I mind my own business, mostly."

"How about Sarah Winslow?" Officer Moy says.

I shake my head. "No, not really. I might have seen her around, but I don't remember. There are many people walking around the building all the time. There's no way I can remember them all. Bradford was memorable because, I guess, he was popular among the students," I say.

"How so?"

"He ..." I pause and think carefully before I say anything. "People always surrounded him. One thing that stood out is that he spoke loudly, and his voice was unavoidable."

"I see. What about Sarah Winslow? Did you have interactions with her?"

"No, sir, I did not."

The officers give each other a brief look and nod at each other.

"As a janitor, do you have access to all the rooms at the university?"

"Yes, sir."

"So, you can unlock any door and enter any room with no problem?"

"That's right, sir," I say with false pride in my voice.

"Did you know that a bottle of cyanide killed Bradford and it was stolen from the chemistry lab?"

I widen my eyes and shake my head. "I ... I didn't know."

Officer Banks furrows his brows and leans forward. "Mr. Smith, I hope you're telling the truth. The whole university knows the cause of the victims' death, and the bottle was missing. How do you not know?"

I shrug my shoulders and tell them with the calmest tone in my voice, "I didn't know it was stolen from the chemistry lab. I'm not the only one who has the keys to all the rooms at the university, sir. There are other janitors working for the university and other administrators have them, too. I wish I could help you with the investigation, but I've told you everything I know."

"Where were you on the night Bradford Robertson and Sarah Winslow died?"

"I believe I was at home." I keep my face straight as an arrow.

"You believe? How certain are you?"

"Sir, I am a family man. I like to stay home with my wife."

Officer Moy nods as if he understands this statement well. Both of them strike me as nice guys, family men, *trying to do the right thing in life. It's a miracle I am married, but I am not immune to love. My wife is several years younger than me, so we hope to have children someday.*

When children come, I will turn my life around and work on becoming a better man.

"Mr. Smith, is there anyone you can think of who could be considered as a suspect involved in the deaths of the two victims?"

I shake my head slowly and purse my lips. "No, not really. I am just a janitor doing my job and trying to feed my family." I shrug my shoulders. I look at Officer Banks straight in the eye to convey the truth.

That statement drives home with them. In their view, I have no motive to kill either the student or the teaching assistant. Their deaths appear to be inconsequential to me. The officers look disappointed as they got no more clues to further probe the mystery of the two cases.

"Mr. Smith, thank you for your time. You're free to go," Officer Moy says.

I nod and stand up from my chair. As I grab the doorknob, Officer Banks' voice startles me. "Mr. Smith."

I freeze, and my body tenses up.

"Please leave the door open behind you."

As soon as I hear those words, my body releases the tension. I nod without turning back. On my way out, I smile and give a small wave to the man at the front desk. He doesn't reciprocate, but it's okay.

It's okay. Everything is okay, because I've gotten away with the crime again.

But there's one more thing I need to do.

I sit in my car and drive away in a familiar direction. I park in the woods and wait for darkness to come. I have everything I need with me, including a salami sandwich I made this morning and a bottle of water. When it gets dark, I leave the woods and drive through the neighborhood until I get there. I park around the corner of the block, take the plastic bag out of the trunk, and walk to the house I've seen many times before. It looks awfully dark, as if no one is inside. That brings me relief, because I don't want him dead. I just want him to suffer a little more, like the way he used to make me suffer.

The next-door neighbor is watching me, so I wave. He waves back and gives me a toothless smile. I walk behind the house to the backyard and place the plastic bag on the ground. The yard is protected by the fence all around, and there's no chance anyone can see me.

I take a bottle of gasoline out of the bag and start pouring it all over the ground. I tap the pockets of my jacket wildly and realize I might have forgotten to bring a lighter. But then I remember it's in the inside pocket. I pull it out and smile.

It feels good and familiar, like in the old days. I ignite the lighter and place it against the gasoline. Fire starts immediately. I stand there for a few more seconds and feel the heat of the fire.

This is the last draw.

Now I can move on from everything. I can finally be even with Whiz.

CHAPTER 45

THE HOUSE IS COLD. I am lying on the couch, shivering. The living room window is still broken, and I can feel the breeze coming through. It doesn't concern me. I don't know how long I've been lying on the couch. I drift in and out of sleep. Every so often, I rise and head to the restroom. My stomach feels glued to my back, and it feels empty. I haven't had a proper meal for a few days.

It's cold and I draw the blanket in, covering my face. The world feels empty, and I'm scared. My thoughts run wild, trying to comprehend what went wrong. Like a horse galloping through a field, my mind races, too. It brings me back to my childhood, my school years, the college years, my marriage. As I reflect on these experiences, I realize I've made a few mistakes in life. Maybe not a few. Maybe a few too many.

But to repent it's too late. I don't know what I can do to start my life anew. What would be the point if I no longer have Emily or the job I once loved and worked so hard to have? It's all utterly hopeless.

My mind races until I smell a fire. I remove the blanket from my face and take a whiff. There's definitely a fire somewhere nearby. I turn to my left and through the window. I notice a blaze outside. Its arms are extending toward me and waving. I wave back and smile in my mind.

The survival instinct kicks in and tells me I should call 911 and report the fire. But I don't move. I can't. I'm paralyzed, but I try not to panic. The fire is spreading quickly. The old man, my neighbor, comes to mind— maybe he will call the police for me to report it. If he doesn't, it won't matter.

I lie back on the couch and put the blanket over my head again. The crackle of the fire is getting closer. I remain silent, still. I close my eyes.

And then I wait.

CHAPTER 46

MITCH'S HOUSE *has burned to the ground. By the time the firetrucks showed up, it was too late. Apparently, his next-door neighbor watched the house go in flame and didn't bother to call nine-one-one. There was a unified hatred for Mitch, and no one wanted to go the extra mile to rescue him.*

Mitch, apparently, didn't call 911 either. I think he chose death rather than attempting to flee the fire. It's not the outcome I expected, but when I think back, this is the only way he could end his misery. In such a short while, it all disappeared—his wife, home, job, honor... what was left to live for? It seemed he wasn't keen on bouncing back and starting anew.

The firefighters found his body in the spot that used to be his living room. It looked like a sizeable piece of chalk lying on the ground, his stature barely recognizable. The town is terrified of the news, but no one seems to be surprised. Everyone thinks he has taken his own life, given all the misfortunes he has suffered lately.

The misfortunes I have orchestrated.

It all started one day when I learned Mitch was a faculty member at a local university. When the news reached me, instant resentment and rage came over me. As he advanced in life to follow a noble profession, I was struggling to make a living. All my life, I have done menial jobs. Initially, I worked as a grocery bagger down the street from my home until I was promoted to a merchant stocker in the warehouse a few months later. They fired me when they caught me stealing a bottle of soda one day. The stealing wasn't intentional. I had just forgotten to pay. But being a lowlife that I was, it was easy to peg me down as an outright petty criminal. I disputed their claim, but I lost. No surprise there. I had had many other jobs since: an auto mechanic assistant, a garbage truck driver, a sewage inspector—none that fulfilled me or paid me well.

I applied to be a janitor at the university and was surprised by how fast they hired me. Even more surprising was the fact that Mitch couldn't remember me when we crossed each other's path for the first time. It offended me at first, but then I thought my plan would go a lot easier. But I did wonder if he still remembered Whiz was his nickname in the middle school. His nickname was inspired by the simple fact he was exceptionally bright, but troubled, like his friend Bulldog.

They both had ruined my life. But now that I was

closer to Whiz, my plan to take revenge on him was a lot easier.

First, Bradford's murder. Choosing him was straightforward because he was a bully.

The day I poisoned Bradford, I knocked on his door room. Not having surveillance cameras in the hallways worked to my advantage. I'd thought I heard someone screaming in the room and wanted to check if everything was alright. Bradford had been studying and looked confused when I inquired. I handed him a cup of coffee mixed with cyanide, telling him this would help with his studies. He smiled at my gesture, said, "thanks, man," took a sip, and closed the door. Fifteen minutes later, I knocked on his door again to check up on him, but there was no response. I knew he was already dead.

I entered his room and found Bradford at his desk, his head resting on the textbook. I walked by him casually and planted the diary I had written as him. All that smack talk about Mitch came from me, not Bradford. I placed the diary on Bradford's bed to ensure the police would find it. When word got around about Bradford's thoughts on Mitch, that's when his reputation declined. All I had to do was sit and watch the ugly things unfold.

But Emily? My biggest high school crush? Back then, I knew having her in my life was like chasing after a dream. Emily's death was a pure accident. Ultimately, Sarah was to blame. I despised her so much so that I killed her. I followed her around for a couple of days to get a sense of her schedule and knew she'd go home around midnight the night I murdered her. It was easy. I was a few steps behind her when I called her name. She turned around and stood there, trying to discern who I was. She couldn't tell, because I wore a face mask. I quickened my steps to reach her and stabbed her with a knife several times. She fell to the ground, bleeding profusely, her eyes staring at me, her brows furrowed. She knew that death was near.

To kill a person and get away with murder is easier than you think. But killing Mitch would have been too simple. I would rather watch him suffer.

And suffer he did.

Now, I'm ready to turn the page. No more hurting people, no more burning down properties. There's a thin line between the aggressor and the victim. Pain breeds more pain. It's a vicious cycle. It gets ugly. I've ruined Mitch's life as much as he has ruined mine. I know two wrongs don't make a right. But when I was in control, when I watched Mitch's life crumble to pieces, I no longer felt a victim.

The cycle ends now, and life, whatever is left of it, needs to go on.

Now, you may ask yourself: who is the real master of demise here?

And my answer?

Well, I think we all are.

THANK YOU!

I sincerely thank you for reading this book!

Please consider leaving a review, even if it's only a sentence, checking out my other books, and subscribing to my website. I'm also happy to answer any questions you may have, so do please get in touch with me via my website:

https://nadijamujagic.com

ABOUT THE AUTHOR

Nadija Mujagić was born and raised in Sarajevo, Bosnia and Herzegovina, what used to be the former Yugoslavia back in the late 1970s. In 1997, she moved to the United States shortly after the end of the Bosnian War and has lived in Massachusetts since. In her spare time, she enjoys playing sports and electric bass guitar. *The Master of Demise* is her sixth book.

ALSO BY NADIJA MUJAGIC

Ten Thousand Shells and Counting: A Memoir

Immigrated: A Memoir

Till a Better World: Woman's Fiction

The Brilliant Mirage: A Thriller

The Exchange: A Psychological Thriller

www.ingramcontent.com/pod-product-compliance
Lightning Source LLC
Chambersburg PA
CBHW051142190726
48290CB00006B/1958